THE DOOMSDAY ARCHIVES

Zack Clark

Nick Eliopulos

THE DOOMSDAY ARCHIVES

The Wandering Hour

THE DOOMSDAY ARCHIVES

The Wandering Hour

ZACK LORAN CLARK & NICK ELIOPULOS

zando young readers

NEW YORK

zando YOUNG reaDers

Copyright © 2024 by Zachary Loran Clark and Nicholas Eliopulos

Zando supports the right to free expression and the value of copyright. The purpose of copyright is to encourage writers and artists to produce the creative works that enrich our culture. Thank you for buying an authorized edition of this book and for complying with copyright laws by not reproducing, scanning, uploading, or distributing this book or any part of it without permission. If you would like permission to use material from the book (other than for brief quotations embodied in reviews), please contact connect@zandoprojects.com.

Zando Young Readers is an imprint of Zando.
zandoprojects.com

First Edition: January 2024

Text and cover design by Carol Ly
Cover art by Chris Shehan
Interior illustrations by Julian Callos

The publisher does not have control over and is not responsible for author or other third-party websites (or their content).

Library of Congress Control Number: 2023933803

978-1-63893-030-3 (Hardcover)
978-1-63893-031-0 (ebook)

10 9 8 7 6 5 4 3 2 1
Manufactured in the United States of America

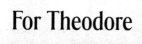

For Theodore

PROLOGUE

New Rotterdam was no place to grow up.

Though Brian Skupp had lived there his whole life, the seaside town still felt vaguely baffling to him, like a knotty vocabulary word he'd looked up multiple times, but his mind could never hold on to.

For one, its narrow, twisted roads were a maze. He frequently found himself confused when straying from the relatively simple route between home and school. It also didn't help that the town was often dense with fog: a soupy mass that arrived with dawn and clung stubbornly to the earth until the sun finally elected to rise and shine and scrub the place clean. *If* it did.

It was an overcast evening, the wind from the Atlantic already bitingly cold. Brian dallied at his locker after band practice, watching as students and teachers rushed home from their after-school activities. He played tuba in band, but not out of any great love for the instrument. Practice just delayed the trip back to his apartment, where he would discover if his father had prepared a meager dinner of boiled hot dogs and instant ramen—or whether it would be up to Brian to feed them both.

Still, he couldn't linger here forever. Though *Brian* might delay, time stalked ever onward. The gray sky grew dimmer, the fog colder. He ambled through the school courtyard, toward the front entrance. The halls were thinning, most of the stragglers having made it to the parking lot. He was just about to do the same when he caught a glimmer at the center of the courtyard.

A strange object sat on one of the stone benches, its gold frame completely at odds with the concrete and iron of Gideon de Ruiter Middle School. Stepping closer, Brian saw that the object was a large hourglass, though much fancier than any he'd seen in person. It was about the size of the marble busts displayed in the local history museum—the pale ghosts of the city's founders captured in stone. Honestly, the hourglass looked like *it* belonged in a museum, not looming atop some public-school bench.

Gilded snakes writhed along its frame, and the glass was filled with a sparkling red sand that was as fine and serous as blood. Curiously, the sand was only gathered in the top bulb.

That didn't make sense. Hourglasses flowed down. Was it broken?

Brian edged closer, then lowered his tuba and squatted to get a better look. It seemed intact—the frame was polished and the glass unblemished by any imperfections that he could see. But sure enough, not a single grain occupied the bottom bulb.

Tentatively, he reached out his hand, fingers nearly brushing the hourglass's tortuous frame.

Brian stopped.

Something about this felt strange, untrustworthy, even—a bizarre object set right where it shouldn't be. It was almost like one of the scary stories from that wiki, the one that nerdy sixth grader Hazel Grey worked on with her friend, the new kid.

New Rotterdam was practically overflowing with local legends and superstitions, but Brian was an eighth grader now, nearly a high schooler. He didn't believe in that stuff anymore. And he had real problems to worry over.

Still, on a day like today, with the clouds churning overhead, some inner part of him shrank from the mysterious object. This felt . . . like a trap.

He lowered his hand.

At the same time, a trickle of red began to thread from the top bulb of the hourglass, sand snaking into the bottom. It curled into a loose spiral that slowly lost its shape.

Then the world stopped.

Brian felt the stillness before he saw it. It was as if some subtle pulse he'd heard all his life—the quiet hum of the universe—had gone silent. He gasped, looking up to find the roiling clouds were now completely motionless. The wind had died as well, far too suddenly. Brian whirled around, searching the school courtyard, where he noticed one of the social studies teachers, Ms. Joanna, standing at the far end.

Something was wrong. Brian didn't know what, but he knew that right now, he didn't want to be alone.

Heart pounding, he hefted his tuba case and rushed toward the teacher, not casting another look back at the strange hourglass. If he had, he'd have seen the trickle of sand continue, the lower bulb slowly filling with twinkling red grains.

Ms. Joanna was digging through her purse, probably retrieving her car keys. But as Brian got closer, he noticed she was strangely static. Unnaturally so. Her eyes were on her purse, her left foot raised as if to take a step. But she didn't take it. Instead, she balanced perfectly in place on one foot, more astonishingly still than even a ballerina could achieve.

"Ms. Joanna?" Brian tried.

She didn't answer. Didn't look at him. She didn't even move.

Which was when Brian saw the keys.

Ms. Joanna must have dropped them while fishing them from her purse. They hung suspended in the air just beneath it, the keys fanned out into a sheepish, toothy smile, as if caught in the act of sneaking away.

But they didn't fall. They *didn't fall*.

"No . . ." Brian muttered. "That's not possible."

He dropped his tuba case and raced for the inside doors, yanking them open. A few kids remained in the halls, but as with Ms. Joanna, each figure was frozen in place. Their mouths gaped open midconversation, their feet balanced in dangling strides.

Somehow, the world had stopped for everyone except Brian.

He took a deep breath, just to prove that he could, and pulled at his hair. He was awake. He was alive. This was real. Brian approached a boy and girl several feet away, seventh graders he dimly recognized as members of the drama club. The girl had swept back her long hair with a hand; it hung suspended in the air like decorative Halloween cobwebs.

Brian laughed. He couldn't help it. This was too bizarre. Too preposterous! Moving back to the door, he peered outside again and was surprised to see his tuba case hanging in midair—frozen in time the moment he dropped it.

"Unreal," he said, laughing again.

His blood curdled the moment he heard a second voice laughing with him.

Slowly, Brian turned. Across the lobby, a figure stood at the end of a long hallway, one in which the lights had already been cut off for the day. Brian squinted. He couldn't make out many details. The figure was tall—a teacher, maybe?—and it was every bit as still as everything else. Until it wasn't.

The figure glided forward in a single, languid movement, rounding and winding as it went, but always pointed in his direction. It tread a circuitous path that felt deceptively hostile to Brian—menace disguised as playfulness. Then, just as suddenly as it'd moved, the figure stopped, still shrouded in darkness.

"Hello?" Brian called, startled by the naked fear in his own voice. "Do you know what's going on? Why is everyone frozen?"

The stranger said nothing, but Brian could feel its eyes on him. He took a step backward, his hip pressing against the push bar that opened the door.

The figure glided slowly forward again, zigzagging into the light, then paused.

It was an old woman. She was white—pale, but most were in a town as gloomy as New Rotterdam—and wore a knit cardigan and jeans. She looked like any number of sweet New England grandmothers, with a halo of gray-white hair and a disarming, if slightly confused, smile. She must be here to pick some kid up from their after-school activities. Still, she looked a bit bewildered to Brian. Like she didn't quite know where she was.

"Are you okay?" he asked. "Do you need help?"

"Help?" the woman repeated back at him.

"I don't know what's going on," Brian said. "But . . . but are you here for someone?"

"Here for someone . . ." the old woman echoed again. "I'm here for *you*, Brian."

She smiled, and Brian noticed for the first time that the woman had too few teeth. What teeth she *did* have were long and thin and needlelike. Almost like . . .

Like fangs.

The woman kept smiling, her grin growing wider and deeper, her teeth longer and sharper. And all this time, she wore the same bewildered expression, even as her jaw unhinged and her mouth gaped open—revealing a ruddy cavity lined in stubby, jagged points.

Brian's feet were moving before his mind had caught up.

He slammed the door open, screaming as he tore through the courtyard, past Ms. Joanna and her suspended keys. Glancing behind him, he caught a blur of movement that wound to his right flank, before curving back around again to his left. It was so fast. Impossibly fast!

He pushed forward, ignoring the dizzying sweeps and curls of whatever hunted him. Soon he burst from the courtyard and into the school parking lot, where dozens of parents and teachers awaited.

Some greeted their children with petrified smiles, while others were packed into idling cars. Steam burped upward from exhaust pipes, suspended in time like morning fog clinging stubbornly past its welcome. The lights were bright, the school's flood beams casting the scene into a strange diorama of families reuniting.

"*Help!*" Brian shrieked at the assembled adults. "Help me, *PLEASE!*"

But none of them turned.

None of them even saw poor Brian as he fled for his life.

Nor did they see the writhing shape that pursued him, curving around his left and striking from the side. It took him in full view of a dozen adults, and no one moved a muscle to help.

New Rotterdam was no place to grow up.

Back in the courtyard, the hourglass flowed—its glittering scarlet sand carefully measuring an hour's worth of time.

When the last grain finally slid through its narrow glass neck, into its gorged belly, there was a subtle sense of movement in the frame. For a moment, it appeared as if the many golden snakes that decorated the hourglass slithered in drowsy circles.

The next moment, the hourglass was gone.

Two sounds immediately echoed across the courtyard. One was a set of keys that jangled to the ground. The other, the bang of a tuba case hitting the pavement.

Brian Skupp, however, was never heard from again.

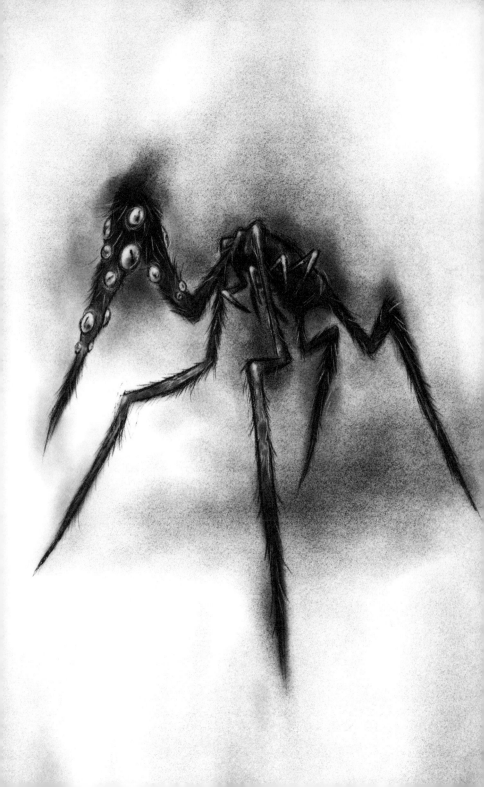

The Long-Necked Dog

From the New Rotterdam Wiki Project

Despite its name, the New Rotterdam cryptid best known as the Long-Necked Dog has never been confirmed as a dog, wolf, or any other canine. Also called the Cold Beach Skulker and Scuttling Rex, it is a stooped and skeletal figure that walks on four needle-thin legs, according to witnesses. It sways back and forth in the air as it moves—as if perpetually off-balance—yet maneuvers with unsettling speed.

The Long-Necked Dog is always sighted at Cold Beach, foraging along the shore after dusk. Its strange, skittering movements have been described as reminiscent of a dock spider, making it easy to spot against the sand in the waning light, even as precise details are more difficult to pick out. Accounts generally agree that it is mottled and dark, and has a long, stooped neck that hangs low to the ground, the origin of its popularized name.

Due to its evasiveness, the cryptid has become something of an unofficial mascot for the Cold Beach waterfront, with many shops along the shore selling T-shirts and hats bearing its striking silhouette.

The Long-Necked Dog unofficial logo

Only one witness has ever claimed to get a close look at the Long-Necked Dog. In the winter of 1991, beachcomber and self-described detectorist Ashton Guyver was scanning the shore with his metal detector when he reportedly came across the creature feeding on a beached shark.

According to Guyver, as his flashlight caught it, the creature raised its long neck, which he purported wasn't a neck at all—but another leg. The "dog," as he claimed, actually had many more than four legs tucked into its body, and many, *many* more than two eyes. Those eyes, he said, glowed with a milky light beneath the flashlight's beam.

Here, Guyver's account becomes confused, a rambling and sometimes contradictory account of the creature *speaking* to him before retreating to a burrow hidden under the docks, dragging the bloated shark behind it. In an interview with local news station WROT-13, he claimed that the Long-Necked Dog told him of a fabulous treasure buried in secret caverns beneath the beach—of gold and jewelry collected over countless years. Guyver welcomed any fellow treasure hunters to join him in looking for an entrance to the caverns, promising to split the riches.

As far as anyone knows, not a single person took him up on his offer—which is probably for the best. Guyver disappeared the next evening after heading off toward the beach alone. Only his metal detector was ever recovered, its sinewy neck bent into a ruin.

1

"It's still too early."

Emrys Houtman sighed from behind his binoculars. He and his friend Hazel were perched on the dunes, peering down at Cold Beach below. They'd been there for an hour already, passing the binoculars back and forth, searching for signs of movement on the sand.

So far, the Long-Necked Dog had yet to appear.

Emrys lowered the lenses and frowned at the horizon, where an enormous thundercloud churned balefully. It was like the sky had grown a great purple eye with which to watch *them*. Lightning flickered between the clouds, made safe and pretty by its distance. But soon enough all that electricity would make it to shore and come crashing down over New Rotterdam.

The town was rainy more often than it wasn't, though this coming storm had made the news. It would be a bad one. Emrys had counted at least a dozen waterfront shopkeepers boarding their windows that afternoon.

"We should get back," Hazel said, as if reading his thoughts. She frowned into the distance, her pale-white face nearly gray under the stormy sky. "The weather's gonna hit before dusk does. We can try another day."

"Yeah . . ." Emrys said dejectedly.

Though Emrys had only recently moved to New Rotterdam, he and Hazel had been friends for years. Sometimes it felt like they shared a brain. They'd met at camp when both were in third grade and formed an immediate bond over their love of scary stories. The moment Emrys was allowed an email account, Hazel had been the very first person he messaged.

He could barely believe it when she'd told him she lived in New Rotterdam, a regular top contender for America's Most Haunted Cities. If Salem was famous for its witches, and New Orleans for its ghosts, New Rotterdam was a hot spot for urban legends. The Laughing Man, Headless Kate, the Shadow in the Mirror—Emrys and Hazel knew all of the city's cryptids and creepypastas by heart.

Even before he'd moved there, Emrys had been an active participant in the New Rotterdam Wiki Project, a shared compendium of supernatural sightings. In fact, it was he and Hazel who'd discovered the lost WROT-13 interview of Ashton Guyver buried in the far reaches of the internet, and added it to the entry for the Long-Necked Dog.

The wiki mods had gone bananas when they saw that. They tore Emrys and Hazel's writing to shreds, of course, but once they'd put it back together again, the two of them were rewarded with special admin status. They could contribute to any entries they liked without restrictions. Emrys had hoped to wow the mods again with an actual sighting today—maybe even a photo—but the cryptid proved elusive.

In fact, he hadn't seen much of anything since moving to New Rotterdam. Sure, the Faceless Founder statue in Centennial Park was creepy, but even after hours of reconnaissance, it hadn't budged an inch. And no matter how many times he rode the carousel at the Foghorn Fairgrounds, Headless Kate never appeared atop the rusty unicorn. At least the popcorn had been good.

Emrys had spent the final weeks of summer before school began combing every supposedly supernatural inch of town— the Shallows shopping district, purported nesting ground of the Orchid from Outer Space; the downtown Five Points District, where one could accidentally stumble through a hidden gate to hell!

So far, he'd remained firmly in the real world. Emrys had to remind himself that was probably for the best.

He stowed his binoculars in his backpack. "Ready?" he asked.

Hazel nodded. They stood and trudged toward the parking lot.

A lone hybrid minivan idled among the empty rectangles painted onto the pavement. Despite being the only person in the lot, Emrys's father had parked perfectly between the lines. He sat now in the front seat, a worn paperback mystery novel propped against the steering wheel.

Though his parents were both avid readers, Emrys had yet to open a book he didn't immediately want to put down. Try as he might to see a forest through the spindly trees of text—to connect with the story, as Emrys's teachers had suggested—his whirring mind always seemed to whir *away* from what he was reading.

It would happen before he even realized he was doing it. One moment he'd be settling into a corner with a steaming cup of honeyed tea, a baggy sweater, and several fluffy pillows—all very cozy, readerly accessories. The next, he'd be at his computer in his underwear, with twenty-seven tabs open on WikiQuery about rising sea levels in the Arctic, a phone game chirping in his lap, and his dog, Sir Galahound, licking bread crumbs from a plate at his feet.

A year ago, Emrys's family doctor had diagnosed him with ADHD—*attention deficit hyperactivity disorder.* At the time, it had summoned to mind images of people bouncing off walls. But Emrys's doctor told him it was actually a common neuro-developmental condition for both kids and adults. ADHD made it hard for Emrys to focus on tasks for very long, especially ones he didn't find interesting.

But on ones he *did* find stimulating, it could have the opposite effect. Sometimes Emrys became hyper-focused—like with the wiki—spending hours on a single task, to the detriment of his other responsibilities. Both were just qualities to keep an eye on.

As he opened the door, Emrys caught the tail end of a news piece about the city's mayor, Selwin Royce. Mayor Royce was giving an interview on the radio.

"I think my record on the environment speaks for itself," he said soothingly. "I love the environment! But I'm not a scientist. I don't think we have enough information to draw any real conclusions on clim—"

Emrys's dad turned the knob, quickly cutting off the sound.

As far as Emrys was concerned, Mayor Royce was the one downside to living in New Rotterdam. Back in Cape Cod, it seemed like their whole town had been dedicated to fighting climate change. Here . . . ?

Mayor Royce epitomized everything Emrys feared about grown-ups and the world they were leaving behind. He fought efforts to move the city to clean energy, and once even sued the New Rotterdam city council for attempting to regulate local vehicle emissions.

Sometimes, when he thought too much about the climate crisis, Emrys found himself struck by an overwhelming feeling of powerlessness, like a great gray tide was pulling him out to sea. How did a kid fight against something like that? He couldn't even vote yet.

So they'd created a new family rule: no Mayor Royce in the apartment. It was a Royce-free zone. An island sanctuary amid the churning waves.

Apparently, the family minivan didn't count.

"Hey, Scoobies," Emrys's dad said as the two of them ducked inside. "Good timing—I was about to come get you. Did you catch the monster terrorizing the beach? Was it Old Man Jenkins in a rubber mask?"

"Dad, nobody gets your weird references," Emrys said, sliding into the front passenger seat. Like his dad, Emrys was white with brown hair. He supposed they looked alike, though Emrys had apparently inherited his mother's eyes. ("And her good judgment—thank the stars," his dad liked to joke with a wink.)

"We appreciate you bringing us here, Mr. Houtman," Hazel said from behind them.

"No problem at all. Who *doesn't* love driving into an approaching superstorm? Though I suppose I'll need the practice, in this town."

"There are *some* nice days," Hazel said. "I think I saw the sun last Wednesday. For a second."

Emrys caught a flicker of something in his dad's expression that was gone before it was really there. He smiled, sealing away an unspoken response. Emrys knew his dad tolerated New Rotterdam, but he hadn't exactly been thrilled when Emrys's mom got the job offer. Renner Houtman had grown up in

California; he liked to joke that his batteries were solar-powered. And while Cape Cod had been bleak in the winter, its bright summers were enough to recharge his depleted reserves.

Emrys's dad didn't make that joke so much anymore. If the last few months were any indication, he'd need to find alternative energy sources. Still, he was loyal enough to Emrys's mom that he held back his complaints. Usually.

"So, what are you two gonna do with your afternoon off?" his dad asked. "Extra credit homework? Pontificate about the meaning of life in the Socratic method?"

"Horror movies!" Hazel cried from the back.

"Horror movies!" Emrys confirmed.

His dad chuckled as the first swollen raindrop splattered against the windshield.

"Don't know how you can watch those things," he said, reversing from the parking spot. "Stiff spines must have skipped a generation. Neither your mom nor I can stand the scary stuff. No, all you got from me is great hair and a sparkling sense of sarcasm."

"Real life is scarier than any movie," Emrys said, watching the line of water slide toward the car hood. "Climate change is real. If monsters are too, then they've done a good job of hiding it. Why be afraid of made-up stuff, when the future is *really* frightening?"

Emrys felt his dad's eyes on him as the car lapsed into silence. Oops.

He'd said something weird again. He hoped it wouldn't result in another family talk about anxiety. Emrys didn't want to *talk* anymore. He wanted to change things, to make the world better. Until that could happen, what use was talking?

A warm hand gripped his shoulder, giving it a squeeze.

"Monsters *are* real, Em," his dad said.

Emrys glanced to his father with surprise.

"They just don't look how we expect them to," he continued. "They're people, like us, who took a wrong step, and then another and another. Until they couldn't even imagine a better path." He gave a wan smile. "But since they're not vampires or werewolves, that also means they're not invincible. It means *other* people—smart, compassionate, clear-sighted people like you—can walk those better paths and set the world straight. Right?"

"Right," Emrys echoed, though he couldn't quite force himself to believe it.

"I bet a stake through the heart would still work on Mayor Royce, though," Hazel chimed in from the back.

As they rounded out of the Cold Beach parking lot, Emrys watched the beachfront gift shops roll past. Ceramic mugs crowded the shelves, each apparently meant to be filled with CRYPTID TEARS. T-shirts boasted I FACED THE FACELESS FOUNDER AND ALL I GOT WAS THIS . . . WAIT, DID YOU HEAR THAT?

Emrys caught sight of a figure in the gloom, shrouded beneath a heavy raincoat. They were holding something—a wooden sign, it looked like—though Emrys couldn't make out the words.

"Who else would be out here with the storm approaching?" Emrys's dad asked. "Think they need help?"

But as the minivan drew closer, the words on the sign came into relief. They'd been spray-painted in blocky red letters.

THE END
IS HERE
AND IT IS
HUNGRY

The figure wore a plague mask beneath the hood of their raincoat, with two goggled eyes and a long, eerie beak that resembled a raven's head.

"Maybe, uh . . . maybe not," Emrys's dad mumbled. He locked the car doors.

Despite the lack of verifiable cryptids, in his short time in New Rotterdam, Emrys had seen all sorts of strange *people*. The town just seemed to draw them in. He turned back to Hazel, his eyes wide. "Something for the wiki?" he asked.

His friend shrugged eloquently. Living there her whole life, Hazel had probably seen hundreds of oddballs like this—macabre tourists come to bask in New Rotterdam's eerie glow.

"It's not really enough for a full entry," she said, "but I'll add it to the Uncanny Sightings talk page. 'The end is hungry'? What does that even mean?"

"Maybe the four horsemen have low blood sugar," Emrys's dad cracked.

Then he pressed down on the gas, quickly leaving the stranger with the sign behind.

The Faceless Founder

From the New Rotterdam Wiki Project

Nobody knows who defaced—as in, literally removed the face from—the statue at the center of Centennial Park.

Originally, the statue depicted New Rotterdam's founding father, Gideon de Ruiter, who is best remembered for leading the town through the deadly winter of 1636. In recent years, de Ruiter has become somewhat controversial, ever since a new biography revealed the role he played in the infamous New Rotterdam Witch Trials.

He was still a hugely popular figure, however, when the statue was erected in 1876. Which made it especially strange that his statue was defaced in 1877, again in 1879, and twice in 1885. Each time, the city council footed the bill for repairs, until, at last, they'd had enough. In 1886, the plaque bearing de Ruiter's name was removed, and city leaders declared that the statue would thereafter represent all of New Rotterdam's many founders, not any one man in particular.

In essence, they said, "We meant for it to look like that."

Time passed, and most people forgot that "The Faceless Founder" ever had a face. The statue was just another oddity in a town that seemed full of them. Its strange story might have been forgotten altogether, but on a dark autumn night in 1991, a man named Albert Rhodes was attacked while jogging through the park. He claimed his assailant had no face. The cuts on Rhodes's cheek and forehead made it clear his assailant *did* have a knife.

Rhodes had barely escaped with his life . . . and he was utterly certain that his attacker had meant to cut his face off.

Some called him a liar. Some claimed he was the victim of a nasty prank.

But there are others who think otherwise—those who believe the spirit of Gideon de Ruiter stalks Centennial Park at night, hoping to find the face that he lost.

And if he can't find it—he'll settle for taking yours.

2

The rain began in earnest a few blocks from home. It announced itself in a steady barrage, knocking relentlessly against the car's roof like a hundred hands seeking entry. Even with the wipers going full bore, Emrys found it difficult to see through the deluge. The road ahead was an obstacle course of indistinct shapes, every one of them a potential danger obscured by rain. He kept his eyes forward, ready to call out if he spotted anything in their path that his father didn't.

Finally, he saw their apartment building rise up through the storm, teetering and distorted, as if viewed from underwater.

Forty-nine Eldridge Heights was an old building. Like many on the block, it was constructed from local sandstone sometime in the early 1900s, by a retired sailor-turned-architect named . . . Something Eldridge. Emrys could never remember. He didn't have Hazel's perfect recall.

Emrys's dad stopped in front of the building so Emrys and Hazel could rush inside. "My kingdom for a driveway," he said. There was no such thing in New Rotterdam—the buildings were all packed in too tightly. Emrys's dad would have to continue driving up and down the crowded streets until he found an empty spot at the side of the road.

"Sorry," Emrys said as he prepared to open his door.

"Hey, don't cry for me," said his dad. "It's too wet out here as it is!"

The sky flashed and thunder roared overhead as Emrys and Hazel ran from the minivan to the building's awning. The water seemed to be coming from everywhere at once, and for a moment, Emrys imagined drowning right there, like the stories of people getting lost and dying in snowbanks mere feet from their homes. He wrestled with the front door, twisting and turning his key to find the lock's elusive sweet spot. Just as he was about to admit defeat and ask Hazel to take over, he felt a click, and the satisfying tilt of stubborn machinery finally conceding.

"Ugh!" Hazel said, her voice echoing in the tiny vestibule as she tugged her sodden T-shirt away from her body. "Fifty-two inches of rain every year, and I think we just got half of it in the last five minutes."

Out of habit, Emrys scanned the handful of packages the mail carrier had left in the vestibule. One in particular caught his eye: a box wrapped in brown paper and adorned with a scattering of colorful stamps. It was addressed to Alyx Van Stavern in apartment #701.

"He got another package," Emrys said.

Hazel knew immediately who he meant. She crouched low for a better look. "It's from Inverness," she said. "That's in Scotland." She picked it up and shook it.

"Careful!" said Emrys. "We don't know what's in there."

"That's what I'm trying to figure out," Hazel said, but she put the package back where she'd found it and started up the staircase. "Sounded like pickled eyeballs to me."

Emrys laughed, falling into step behind her. "What do pickled eyeballs even sound like?"

"Same as normal eyeballs," Hazel answered, and she rapped her knuckles against door #304. "But pickling keeps them from spoiling on a transatlantic flight."

"If you say so," Emrys said. "But you'd think he could pickle eyeballs in the comfort of his own home and save a lot of money on shipping."

Their friend and neighbor Serena opened the door to her apartment while Emrys was midsentence. She arched an eyebrow pretty much immediately. "Do I want to know what you're talking about?"

"The Sorcerer of #701 got a package," Hazel said breezily. She stepped inside without waiting for an invitation, while Emrys stood dripping on the welcome mat. Hazel and Serena had lived at 49 Eldridge Heights for years—since they were babies. They had the easy familiarity of lifelong pals. And while Emrys and Hazel had been fast friends, he was still getting to know Serena. They hadn't clicked in quite the same way.

Of course, she could afford to be choosy. From what Emrys had gathered, Serena had a lot of friends. He occasionally heard them giggling on their way up or down the stairwell, and Serena's bedroom wall was a veritable collage of group photos—high-spirited birthday parties, campground gatherings, and crowded selfies.

Emrys, by contrast, had never had more than a handful of friends at one time. He liked to think of it as a matter of quality over quantity, but the truth was simply that some people—most people—thought he was a weirdo. He knew how lucky he was to have found Hazel, and if Hazel and Serena were inseparable, then he would be as friendly as possible to Serena and hope for the best. Even if Serena could be . . . prickly.

"Ah, ah, ah," Serena said, raising a hand to stop Hazel's advance. "My dads will not be happy if you drip all over their floor like a couple of wet dogs. They just had it refinished."

"Then it should be protected against water damage, right?" said Hazel.

"Let me get you a towel, smart girl," Serena said, already stooping to open a strange cupboard with a large, grooved piece of metal—like a giant screw—set into its wooden frame. It put Emrys in mind of a medieval torture device.

"*That's* new," said Hazel.

"On the contrary," said Serena. "It is ridiculously old. But somehow Mr. Pierce convinced my parents that what this apartment really needed was a three-hundred-year-old linen press."

She handed them each a towel. "The amount of money they spend in his shop, I think he must have them hypnotized. Maybe *he's* a wizard. Should we snoop through his mail, do you think?"

"Serious inquiries only, please," said Hazel.

"Van Stavern's package is from Inverness," Emrys said, blotting the rainwater from his arms. "In Scotland!"

"Ah, it makes sense now," Serena said, tapping her chin theatrically. "He's the love child of Nessie and a leprechaun."

Hazel rolled her eyes. "Leprechauns are Irish."

"Leprechauns are make-believe!" Serena said. "And the 'Sorcerer of #701' is a sad old man with no family. Leave him be."

Hazel looked back at Emrys and shrugged. It's not as if they'd ever dream of bothering the man. It was fun, though, to have a little bit of mystery right there in their apartment building.

Emrys had never even seen Alyx Van Stavern, aside from a fleeting glimpse of a sour face peering down from the top-floor window on moving day—a face that was quickly replaced with drawn curtains. When he'd asked Hazel about the man who lived in the penthouse apartment, her eyes had grown wide.

She'd told him what little she knew of the strange recluse who'd moved in a year before and had rarely—if ever—left his apartment since. He hadn't even answered the door when Hazel had trudged upstairs with her mother's "welcome to the neighborhood" casserole, although she was certain he'd been home. She'd smelled an odd odor coming through his door, like old eggs. On another occasion weeks later, she'd heard a howl, like an animal in pain, coming from upstairs, but her mother claimed it was just an alley cat on the roof. Aside from that, the only sign that the man existed was the steady influx of packages bearing postmarks from all over the world—Budapest and Sighişoara and Château de Brissac—which the building's super, Mr. Popov, carried upstairs and left on the seventh-floor landing. (Hazel had asked.)

Emrys found himself composing, expanding, and revising an imaginary wiki entry on their local "Sorcerer of #701" with each new piece of information he gleaned. Of course, he wouldn't actually submit an entry that was 100 percent hearsay and speculation. He took the site too seriously for that. The mods were counting on him.

"My dads are at some party, but they left us a frozen pizza," Serena said, and she took their damp towels and motioned for them to come inside. "My brother's at his friend's house. So the apartment is ours for the night. I've got a super gory movie picked out already. You'll love it."

"Your parents are out?" said Emrys. "In the storm? Aren't you worried?"

Serena flicked her wrist as if batting the suggestion away. "This is New Rotterdam," she said. "If I worried about rain, I'd be worried all the time. And what fun would that be?"

Emrys forced himself to chuckle, but hardly any sound came out. *Worried all the time. No fun.* Was that directed at him?

"Oh! You haven't told me yet," said Serena, as she sat side-ways in a big reclining chair, draping her legs over the side. "How was your little adventure? Did you get photographic proof of the long-limbed dog?"

"It's the Long-*Necked* Dog," Hazel corrected. Less fiercely, she added, "And . . . no. Not this time."

"We were too early," put in Emrys.

"Yes." Serena sniffed. "I'm sure that was the problem."

Serena's movie selection was as gruesome as she promised—a bloody affair in which a group of teenagers were eliminated one by one by a mysterious knife-wielding assassin. Serena laughed at every demise, relishing the over-the-top effects and the dark humor, while Hazel pointed out the plot holes and continuity errors. Emrys spent half the movie reading spoilers on his phone. Even armed with knowledge of what was going to happen, he watched the scariest parts through his fingers.

By the time the killer was revealed—improbably enough, the culprit was the comatose prom queen, who held supernatural sway over her classmates—it was well and truly dark outside. The sun had been hidden by clouds all afternoon, and at some point, it had sunk, unseen, below the horizon. The night, as black as the day had been gray, was lit only by irregular flashes of lightning and the yellow glow of electric lights on the street below.

None of them were prepared for the shrieking of the door buzzer, which cut through the night like a deranged prom queen's cleaver, making bloody tatters of the quiet.

Hazel screamed, causing Serena to spill the popcorn (which was mostly buttery kernels by that point). Emrys fell right off the couch.

Serena slapped Hazel's arm playfully. "You scared me!"

"Not on purpose!" Hazel squeaked.

"Who is it?" Emrys wondered aloud.

"It's probably my brother," Serena answered. "He forgets his keys all the time."

Their apartments all had the same simple intercom system— a beige control panel with a speaker and three buttons, mounted on the wall beside each apartment's door. Serena sauntered up to the panel and pressed the "speak" button. "Who is it?" she asked in a singsong voice. She pressed the "listen" button so that they could hear the reply.

But there was no reply.

She tried again. "Helloooo?" she said. "Dom, is that you?"

No answer. Just the low hiss of the speaker, and the faint staccato tap of rain on pavement. And maybe . . .

"Do you hear—?" Emrys began.

"Shh!" said Serena.

They all leaned closer to the intercom. The sound quality was so poor that Emrys couldn't be sure, but he thought he heard . . .

Breathing.

Serena quickly pulled her hand away from the panel. "Did you guys hear that?" she whispered. "Someone's down there."

"Maybe it's Dom, like you said," Hazel suggested. "He's probably messing with us."

"Forget *that*," Serena said, and she jammed the "speak" button. "Hey, weirdo!"

Emrys flinched. That word always stung like an insect bite.

"We don't want any," Serena continued. "Go bug somebody else, all right? Get lost!"

Emrys's jaw dropped, and Hazel said, "Wow."

Serena took her finger off the button and did her patented shrug-and-smirk combo. "That should take care of that. Now, can we *please* go finish the—"

A sudden burst of strobing light flashed in the windows, filling the apartment with searing brightness; a roaring crash of thunder followed quickly after, seeming to shake the whole building. They all yelped in surprise, then yelped again when the lights cut out and the apartment was plunged into darkness.

"Well, crap," said Serena.

"I can't see!" said Emrys. The dazzling flash of lightning had set his vision buzzing. He flailed about, accidentally smacking Hazel in the face.

"None of us can," Hazel said, batting away his hand. "Give it a minute."

There was a moment of absolute silence as they waited for their eyes to adjust. Emrys checked his pockets for his phone, then realized he'd left it on the couch.

And then the door buzzer, right beside them, shrilled loudly.

This time, Hazel didn't scream. Or maybe she did, and Emrys simply couldn't hear it. This close, the buzzer was so *loud*—he clapped his hands to his ears, desperate for the sound to stop, but it kept going in a long, uninterrupted shriek.

Suddenly, a light cut through the void. Hazel found her phone and activated her flashlight app, and now the entryway was lit in a harsh blue-white light. The shadows moved at severe angles as she swung the phone around to illuminate their surroundings. Emrys saw Serena pounding her fist against the intercom in a vain attempt to make it stop. When it became clear that wasn't working, Serena gripped it with both hands— and ripped it off the wall.

The noise stopped immediately.

"Dang," Emrys said, and his voice sounded weirdly faint in his ringing ears. "What was that about?"

"These stupid things are older than my parents," Serena said brightly. "Now we'll get a new one. I did us a favor!"

Hazel was quiet. She peered at the space where the intercom had been. Emrys followed her gaze and saw a few small wires sticking out from a hole in the wall.

"I'll get some candles," Serena said, already walking across the room. Peering out a window, she said, "It looks like the neighbors still have power. Was our building struck by lightning?"

Emrys undid the dead bolt and opened the door. He could make out Serena's welcome mat, and beyond it, the very edge of the stairwell. Past the boundary of Hazel's light, however, all was pitch black. "The whole building's dark," Emrys said. He turned to Hazel, whose brows were screwed up in worry. "What's wrong?" he asked.

"Nothing," she said. "It's just . . . the buzzer went off *after* the power went out. But don't the intercoms use electricity?"

Before Emrys had a chance to process her question, he heard something out there in the dark.

It was the sound of the door downstairs—the entrance to the building, on the ground floor. There was no jangle of keys; no grinding of the ancient, stubborn lock.

Just the *click* of the opening door, and the *clack* as it fell back into place.

And then, the sound of someone whistling.

Hazel locked eyes with Emrys. Her hand shook, and the light shook with it, making the shadows on her face twist and bend. Neither of them said anything; they both held their breath and listened.

Click, click came the sound of footfalls in the stairwell.

Click, click. The cheerful whistling continued, the notes bright and clear.

Click, click. The melody was familiar—wasn't it? Yet Emrys couldn't quite place it.

Click, click. Whoever it was, they had made it to the second-floor landing.

Maybe they'd stop there. Maybe—

Click, click. No. No, they were still coming.

Click, click. Pretty soon Emrys would be able to see them. Whoever was whistling, they'd be coming around the bend in the staircase in just another moment. He peered into the darkness beyond Hazel's light, which bobbed unsteadily, casting writhing, distorted shadows beyond the threshold. He gripped her wrist to steady the light; he squinted to get a better look . . .

Hazel quickly but quietly closed the door.

"What *was* that?" Serena edged back toward them, but Hazel shushed her, and slowly slid the dead bolt into place as silently as she could. Then she turned off her light, plunging them back into darkness.

Emrys couldn't see anything, but his hearing seemed to sharpen with fear.

He could hear his heart pounding in his chest.

He could hear Hazel, breathing raggedly beside him.

And he could hear that whistling—that pretty, melodic, cheerful whistling—as the whistler walked past Serena's door and up, up, up the winding staircase.

The Nightingale Box

From the New Rotterdam Wiki Project

The earliest record of the Nightingale Box comes from the journal of Liu Feng Chao, a young fishing trawler whose family relocated to New Rotterdam from Santa Barbara in the 1880s. An amateur poet and meticulous diarist, Liu Feng wrote of finding a strange puzzle box amidst his catch one morning, describing it as "a sealed cell of bronze, wood, and glass." He noted that he would occasionally hear musical trills from within, as if a songbird were trapped inside.

The next several entries of Liu Feng's diaries catalog his frustrated attempts at opening the box. The aspiring poet was sure that cracking the lock mechanism would free the "pure inspiration" captured within. Each time he solved one of the puzzle's components, Liu Feng claimed he was rewarded with bursts of creative insight. Indeed, of his collected poems, the ones written during this period are widely considered his best. "Drowned Nightingale," written just a day before his death, has been described by the New Rotterdam Cultural Institute as "*the* poetic masterpiece of its time."

Sadly, Liu Feng didn't live to see his own success. The night after he wrote what would be his seminal work, the young poet's family reported hearing excited cries of triumph from his bedroom, "which quickly turned to anguished screams." They found Liu Feng dead in his room, his expression a gruesome mix of terror and elation.

The Nightingale Box disappeared that night, but has resurfaced many times over the years, often to famous (and famously short-lived) New Rotterdam artists, including painter Ken Gleeman, singer/songwriter Infra Red, dancer Ginger Perez, and Andy Warhol–contemporary Quoi. All died under mysterious and grisly circumstances, just as their creative outputs blossomed.

Its most recent sighting was in a 1999 MTV interview of up-and-coming VJ Mason Weekly in his New Rotterdam beachfront home. In the interview, a visibly distracted Weekly frequently glances toward what appears to be an ornate container lined with metallic dials. A warbling tune can occasionally be heard in the background audio. Weekly died three days after the interview, walking fully clothed into the sea. Witnesses' reports conflict on whether his rictus grin was gleeful or despairing.

3

The darkness was smothering. Even as his eyes adjusted, Emrys found he could barely pierce the gloom. The three of them sat quietly on Serena's sofa, speaking only in terse whispers as they listened for signs of the mysterious whistling stranger. Emrys stayed glued to his phone the whole time. The small pane of light was a window, truer and more farseeing than any real one. It told him the world outside still existed, despite what this claustrophobic darkness might have him believe.

Emrys knew he'd need the phone's flashlight to get back to his apartment (*slow footfalls on the stairwell—click, click*), but he couldn't seem to force himself to put it away. He watched with mounting anxiety as his battery life dwindled to forty-nine percent, then thirty-five, then twenty-two, then seven.

He was only saved by the arrival of Serena's dads.

"What. In the world. *Happened?*" Mr. Dubose called once he opened the door. "Serena!"

Serena winced at her father's voice. Mr. Dubose was her bio-dad. Both were Black and had a lot in common: grace, charm, intelligence. They also—Emrys had already discovered in his brief time in the building—could rile one another up like no one else.

"I guess he noticed the intercom," she sighed, pulling on a twist of hair. "I knew Scotch tape wouldn't do it."

Thankfully, Mr. Navarro, Serena's other dad, was there to petition for calm. He entered after Mr. Dubose, with Dom, Serena's brother, just behind him.

"Wuh-huh-ho!" Dom exclaimed with a laugh. "Serena, you've really outdone yourself this time. *Nice* work." Dom breezed past the group and into kitchen, then poked his head out with a grin. "You sure you don't want to take up lacrosse? Most of the new players aren't *half* as sturdy as these intercoms."

"Shut *up*, Dom!" Serena groaned.

"Language," Mr. Navarro interjected patiently. He turned to Emrys and Hazel. "How about we let them burn off some steam, huh?" he said, nodding to the front door. "I'll walk you home."

Mr. Navarro was Dom's bio-dad, and while the two shared his Dominican ancestry and warm brown skin, they were about as different as could be. At least Emrys thought so. Whereas Felix Navarro was kind and thoughtful and soft-spoken, Dom was . . . a handful. He was older than Serena by a couple years, and sometimes he even acted like it. Other times he was like a five-year-old in the body of an eighth-grade linebacker.

Emrys and Hazel nervously followed Mr. Navarro out, but there was no sign of anything strange in the hallway. No blood spatters, or dribbles of monstrous goo, or knife marks scratched into the walls. Emrys's mind ran through all the New Rotterdam legends he could think of, trying to connect one to what he'd heard. The Laughing Man? The Nightingale Box? None of them quite fit. Still, something about the eerie whistling—a bright, cheerful melody that hovered just at the edge of familiarity—had set his already active imagination training for the Anxiety Olympics.

Whoever the mysterious whistler was, they'd somehow gotten into the building without being buzzed. And Emrys hadn't heard them leave.

But the climb home was uneventful. The stairs were the same stairs, just darker, and Emrys could hear muted conversations from the other apartments. If anyone else in the building had noticed the whistling stranger, they didn't seem particularly disturbed.

As Hazel arrived at her door, she turned and said goodbye with a little wave. Emrys offered to ask his parents if she could stay over during the blackout. Hazel's mom was a nurse at Saint Azazel Hospital's emergency room, and her shifts often took place overnight. Hazel hadn't talked much about it during their time at camp, but since moving to New Rotterdam, Emrys couldn't help but notice his friend was frequently home alone.

Still, Hazel demurred, saying she had some cleaning to do.

Then, before Emrys knew it, he was home. His dog, Sir Galahound, greeted him with his usual wiggly butt and waggly tail, before turning his exuberance on Mr. Navarro. Emrys's mom appeared from around the corner, her face outlined in candlelight, just as the dog was receiving an epic ear-scratching.

"Felix!" she said. "Thanks for walking Emrys up. I was just on the verge of getting nervous."

"No problem at all," Mr. Navarro said. "Serena had . . . an accident with the intercom, which is apparently no longer connected to our wall. Figured she and Max could use some space to talk it out."

Emrys's mom grimaced. "Want to come in for a minute? Have a drink?"

"Desperately," Mr. Navarro chuckled. "Thanks, Grace, but I should head back down and offer support. I'll figure out to whom when I get there."

After bidding his parents and Mr. Navarro good night, Emrys hurried to his room, Sir Galahound hot on his heels. He quickly dug the portable battery charger from his desk drawer and connected it to his phone. Instantly, the battery icon in the upper corner was cut in half, bisected by a zig-zagging lightning bolt. That beautiful symbol meant power was flooding into the phone. Everything would be okay.

Outside, thunder boomed. Real lightning was still crashing above New Rotterdam, of course. The storm raged on, but here in 49 Eldridge Heights—with his phone and his dog and his parents readying for bed across the apartment—Emrys finally felt his anxiety begin to disentangle.

Then his phone buzzed.

Did you see anything on your floor? Hazel had texted Emrys and Serena in a group chat.

What do u mean?

The whistler! Hazel texted. *Any sign of them?*

Emrys chuckled. *The Whistler is a pretty good wiki name but no.*

A few moments later, Serena chimed in.

They must have gone all the way up

Was it the Sorcerer of #701? Emrys texted. Then, *Are you in trouble Serena?*

Yes

A beat later, she texted, *Van Stavern never leaves his apartment. Mr. Popov even brings his mail up. Definitely not a whistler.*

He's never had a visitor before, Hazel texted. *Not that I've seen.*

An idea was simmering in Emrys's mind, a pressure that begged for release. It was ridiculous, really. He was already safe in his room in his pajamas, the eeriness of the night long past.

I could listen outside his door, he texted. *Maybe the Whistler went inside?*

Serena was probably right—Alyx Van Stavern probably *was* just a sad old man—but the failure at Cold Beach had left Emrys hungry for a win. What if he discovered a brand-new entry for the wiki? Of the three of them, Emrys was the closest to the Sorcerer of #701's apartment. The man lived just one floor above him. Emrys's parents were in their own bedroom, their door already closed. He was sure he could sneak out and then back in without being noticed.

YES!! Serena texted immediately, just as Hazel's *Emrys no,* popped into the chat below it.

His feet were already on the floor, his fingers tapping frantically. *Just up and down really quick i'll let you now if i hear any thing*

Sir Galahound raised his head, then hopped off the bed, too, curious about the late-night flurry of activity.

"Sorry, boy," Emrys whispered. "I'll be right back."

He decided to forgo his shoes for the mission. Socks would be quieter on the stairs.

The apartment was pitch black—and dead quiet. Emrys tiptoed down the hall to the front door. Thankfully, his parents' room was at the other end of the apartment.

Emrys carefully nudged the door open. He clicked the toggle that allowed it to be opened from the outside without a key, then slipped into the hall and pulled it shut behind him. Only then did he dare turn on his phone's flashlight.

Emrys swung the beam toward the stairway, pointing up to the penthouse apartment that took up the entire seventh floor.

He edged toward the staircase, listening for any signs of conversation—and especially for that eerie, musical whistling. He didn't hear a thing.

Not for the first time, Emrys wondered what he was doing. Just moments ago, the darkness had been so all-consuming, so *confining*, that he could feel his mind rattling against it like a caged animal. Emrys had never been good at sitting still. Quiet moments were when his brain rebelled, conjuring every fear he had ever harbored and holding it up for him to examine. He needed a puzzle to solve, a mystery to worry over, in order to feel truly calm.

Serena loved her slashers, and Hazel her monster movies. Emrys's favorite had always been cosmic horror—stories of forbidden and dangerous knowledge, where characters sought the hidden mysteries of the universe, usually to their dooms. J. B. Goodheart, his favorite writer of the genre, had even grown up near New Rotterdam! Several of the more famous wiki entries—like the Witch's Needle and Five-Pointed Fright—bore striking similarities to Goodheart's stories. Emrys had only seen the movies, of course, but he still sensed a fellow pessimist in the man. Goodheart seemed to suspect that the universe was as cruel as it was vast, and that it only became crueler the more one learned.

Still, just like the ill-fated knowledge seekers of the genre, Emrys found he could seldom leave well enough alone. There was nothing more irresistible than a forbidden question.

He took a careful step up, then another. The beam from his light wobbled as he climbed, sending shadows careening. Darkness warped the shapes around him, twisting every curve into a sinister smile.

Which is perhaps why he didn't notice what was *truly* wrong until it nearly hit him in the face.

A lance of heat plunged through the air, sizzling just past Emrys's nose. Something hissed against the ground, right beside his unprotected foot. Emrys gasped, snapping the flashlight downward, where he saw what appeared to be a boiling bubble of . . .

"Glass?" Emrys rasped aloud.

Instantly, he flicked his phone upward to where a small, old-fashioned light fixture had been set above the landing. Now it was a melted ruin.

Not just the fixture, but the bulb itself. The glass drooped, fusing into the bronze-colored fixture.

Had the building actually been struck by lightning? Surely someone would have noticed. Emrys pointed his light toward the door to apartment #701.

Only there was no door to be found.

There was a door*frame*—or pieces of it, anyway—clinging limply to the wall. But the door itself had been blasted inward by some devastating force. Beyond it was a void, just a rectangle of depthless black. Van Stavern's apartment was so dark, not even Emrys's flashlight penetrated beyond the threshold.

What in the *world* had happened here? And how had no one heard a thing while it was happening? Whatever destroyed this door must have been colossal. Wrecking balls usually made a *noise* when tearing through peoples' homes.

This . . . this was bad. Certainly it was more serious than Emrys could handle on his own. He needed to call the police. Or an ambulance. He needed to *warn* someone.

He took a step back.

"Don't scream," a voice whispered in his ear. Then someone wrapped their hands around his mouth.

The Witch's Needle

From the New Rotterdam Wiki Project

When nine-year-old Gabby Filmore came home with a puppy, her parents weren't happy.

And they were even more upset when she told them she'd found it in the Witch's Needle.

The Witch's Needle is one of New Rotterdam's most recognizable landmarks. It's a thirteen-foot-tall obelisk—like a miniature Washington Monument—carved from a single piece of sarsen stone. That's the same stuff Stonehenge is made of.

According to legend, Sarah Blackthorne, a victim of the New Rotterdam Witch Trials, used the Witch's Needle as a hiding place for her potions and poisons. Her final fate was sealed when Gideon de Ruiter uncovered her hidden flasks and phials in a secret compartment within the monument's hollow base.

That secret compartment would be used again. History tells us that colonists hid ammunition and explosives within it, allowing them to get the drop on an occupying force of redcoats in the bloody insurrection known as the Founders Day Miracle.

Centuries later, smugglers of the Prohibition era used the compartment to hide their illegal moonshine.

There's just one problem with those stories. In 1986, scientists studying the obelisk concluded that *there is no hidden compartment in the Witch's Needle.* Their scans proved that the obelisk is solid stone from tip to base. Those old stories . . . were just stories.

So how did Gabby Filmore find a puppy there in 1993?

Maybe she made up the story. Maybe she found the puppy in a playground or a parking lot and decided to tell a white lie to win her parents over.

We'll never be able to ask her. Because Gabby and her family went missing a few short weeks after she brought that puppy into their home.

Police found the dog sleeping contentedly in Gabby's empty bed. The Filmores, however, were never found.

4

E mrys screamed.

It was an honest scream, high-pitched and undignified and completely involuntary—his body's way of saying it was terrified before his brain even had a chance to process the fear.

Or to process the voice he'd heard.

"I said *don't* scream," hissed that voice. *Serena's* voice. Emrys sagged with relief.

"I warned you not to sneak up on him," whispered Hazel. "I don't know what you—whoa." She noticed the lack of door in Van Stavern's doorframe. "What happened?"

"Something bad," Emrys said.

Hazel squatted down and picked up a broken shard of door. Emrys watched as it fell apart in her fingers, crumbling to dust.

"I-I didn't . . ." Hazel's eyes found his. "You saw that, right? What would do that to a hardwood door?"

"We should call the police," Emrys said.

Serena tutted. "The police? I wouldn't."

"Serena, I love you and I respect your whole anti-authoritarian thing," said Hazel, and she brought her phone up to her ear. "But there's a time and a place, and I'm already calling them."

Emrys turned to Serena. "What do you have against the police?"

Serena didn't look at him. She was peering into the dark doorframe. "Let me guess. Where you come from, it's all Officer Friendly and pals, right?" She shook her head. "Not in this city. You'd better hope they don't pin this on *you*, Mr. First-on-the-Scene."

Emrys was sure she was joking. Or at least exaggerating.

He was pretty sure.

But he felt his heart racing at the idea. They'd certainly have a lot of questions for him. His parents would, too.

Hazel lowered her phone. "It's, uh . . . it's *busy*."

"Try nine-one-one," Emrys suggested.

"I did," Hazel replied.

"I'm sorry, what?" said Serena. "Nine-one-one is *busy*?" She threw up her hands. "This city, I swear!"

"I'll try again," Hazel offered. "It's probably because of the storm."

"We have to go inside. He might need our help." It was Emrys who said it, without fully meaning to. He was usually careful about what he said, hesitant to put forward his ideas and opinions. But now wasn't the time to sit back and compose wiki entries in his head about eerie whistling and disintegrating doors. Their neighbor might be hurt in there.

"We don't have time to wait for somebody else," he said. "Right now, every second counts."

Hazel and Serena shared a look. Emrys couldn't read whatever passed between them, but then they both nodded.

"Yeah, okay," said Serena.

"After you?" said Hazel.

Despite his bold words, Emrys found it difficult to take that first step over the threshold. His phone's light did a poor job of penetrating the inky blackness—he saw more bits of shattered door inside, and a faded rug, and not much else—and there was still the small, panicked voice in his head that knew he was breaking the rules. Even if this was the right thing to do—and it was, he was sure of it—he still found it hard to step outside the lines.

"You've got this," Hazel said at his back, and she shone her light over his shoulder, adding its brightness to his own. "We're right behind you."

The light switch didn't work (because of course it didn't), and as Emrys swung his light around the apartment, he felt a momentary thrill of fear—as if some part of him fully expected to find something crouching there in the dark, waiting for them. He held his breath, searching the shadows for the toothy rictus of the Laughing Man or the luminous cat eyes of Creeping

Ginny. But his light revealed only a large, high-ceilinged room—and glimpses of a truly tremendous mess.

"It looks like thirty to fifty wild boars came through here," he whispered.

"That's weirdly specific," said Hazel. "But true. Watch out for broken glass. Where are your shoes?"

Hazel shone her light at their feet, where chunks of the door lay among shards of glass and ceramic. She followed the trail of glittering debris with her light; it led to a kitchenette set against a nearby wall. The contents of its emptied cupboards seemed to be the source of the broken glass.

"His kitchen's in his living room," Hazel said.

"It's a loft," said Serena. "One big room instead of several little ones."

Good, Emrys thought. *Fewer walls for a knife-wielding killer to be lurking behind.*

"Um, hello?" Emrys called. A floorboard creaked loudly beneath his foot, but his voice came out quiet and small.

"Mr. Van Stavern?" Hazel tried. "Are you here, sir? We're from downstairs."

"Call him Alyx," Serena insisted. "He's our neighbor, not our teacher."

With Serena adding her light to theirs, Emrys was finally able to see the full extent of the vandalism. The mess was staggering. Two couches had been torn open and gutted, their fluffy innards strewn all over. The drawers of the wardrobe and dresser were overturned, clothing piled in heaps.

But books accounted for most of the mess. There were more than a hundred of them, spread out all over the floor with their spines cracked and pages bent.

"My dads would have a heart attack," said Serena. She leaned over to read the spines. "Blake. Crowley. Alan Moore? I'm sensing a theme."

"Mr. Van Stavern?" Emrys cried, urgency bringing more volume to his voice. "Anyone? Hello?"

Serena poked her head into the bathroom—nothing there, she indicated with a curt head movement—while Hazel shone her light into a little alcove where a bed lay empty, its mattress practically turned inside out.

"There's nobody home," said Serena, and Emrys thought she meant it to be good news. If Van Stavern had been out when this had happened, then the old man was probably safe. But Van Stavern almost never left his apartment. Why would he go out in the storm? Emrys tilted his light up at the ceiling, as if the man's body might be stashed in the rafters. They were missing something; he felt it in the pit of his clenched stomach.

"Hey, check this out." Hazel picked something up from the pile of books. "Is this a Ouija board?"

Emrys walked over for a closer look, and a floorboard creaked. Had their neighbor used a spirit board to pierce the veil between life and death? Maybe he'd lost someone he loved—a spouse, or a cherished sibling—and as he'd withdrawn from the world, retreating into his penthouse apartment, his sole comfort had been conversing with the dead. Seances!

He caught Serena giving him a judgmental look and tamped down his enthusiasm. He'd probably looked a little too gleeful as he'd crossed the room, particularly since the object in Hazel's hands turned out to be wholly unremarkable.

"They sell those things at the toy store." He frowned and retrieved the board's matching planchette from the debris at Hazel's feet. "No self-respecting spiritualist would use this. It's plastic. Mass produced." He kicked around in the piles of books. "So much for the Sorcerer of #701. There's nothing here but a Rider-Waite tarot deck and a bunch of crystals and a cheap-looking gargoyle from a gardening store. It's all kind of . . . cheesy."

"Well, what did you honestly expect?" asked Serena. She turned her gaze from Emrys to Hazel. "Both of you. You didn't think this old man is really a wizard?"

"No," said Emrys, his shoulders drooping lower. "Maybe. I don't know."

"Weirder things have happened," Hazel said, defiant in the face of Serena's skepticism. "There's evidence of witchcraft in New Rotterdam dating back hundreds of years."

Emrys shook his head. "Serena's right. Of course she is. Van Stavern is just an old man." He sighed. "He's probably lonely.

People think he's weird because he believes in New Age crystal healing or whatever." He cast his tired eyes around the room. "And somebody came here and they . . . they tore his whole life apart."

"The Whistler," Hazel said with a shiver. "That's who did this. Right? Were they looking for something? I swear I felt a chill as they passed Serena's door. Like someone was stepping on my grave." She nudged Emrys, trying to draw him out of his dark mood. "Maybe it was a rival warlock . . ."

"Or a mob enforcer," Serena suggested. "Perhaps ol' Alyx has a weakness for casinos."

Emrys was no longer in the mood to speculate. Standing amidst the carnage of Alyx Van Stavern's life, he felt a strange sort of kinship with the man—a lonely outsider who surrounded himself with occult-adjacent novelties. The sadness of that realization threatened to overwhelm him.

And in the silence of that moment . . . he heard something.

Hazel noticed his agitation immediately. "What is it?"

Emrys held up a finger. He wasn't certain . . . he needed to be sure . . .

There. He heard it again. It was unmistakable.

"I hear someone *breathing*," he whispered.

"What?" said Serena. "No way. Where?"

"Shh!" said Hazel. She hurried to the bathroom, checking behind its open door. Emrys pressed his ear to a wall.

"I don't hear anything," complained Serena, and as she paced, the floor groaned in protest. "Except this obnoxious floor-board! Is it loose or what?"

Her words jolted Emrys like an electric shock. "The floor-board?" Emrys said, looking down. "We don't have floors like this in my apartment."

Hazel bounced on the balls of her feet. "Our floors are vinyl. This one is made of *planks*. It's like being in a log cabin. Or on a ship . . ."

Emrys leapt over a pile of books, skidding to a stop beside Serena. "Which one's the creaky floorboard?" he asked, but he didn't wait for an answer, dropping to his knees and pressing his ear to the ground.

There it was. Ragged breathing. *Someone was under the floor.*

He looked up at Hazel, and he didn't have to say a word. The horror of his discovery was written all over his face, and his friend immediately joined him on the ground.

"It's loose," she said, prying her fingers between two planks. "We need, like, a crowbar . . ."

"I forgot mine at home," Serena said, but she crossed the room and tore an ornamental sword from the wall. Emrys pegged it for a Renaissance Faire souvenir. Not a *real* sword, but it would be sturdy enough to give them leverage.

Serena stabbed the sword between the planks—"Careful!" Emrys cried—and then she pushed down on it like a lever. The board popped free, the nails giving little resistance, as if this piece of floor had been removed and replaced many times before.

Emrys braced himself for his first glimpse of what was hidden below. He hadn't stopped to wonder what he might see.

But he certainly hadn't expected to find another book.

"What?" he said. "I don't—I swear I heard—"

"What *is* it?" Hazel asked.

Emrys lowered his hands into the rift and brought the book out into the light. It was bound in dark leather, and it bore no title on its cover or spine. Its only identifying mark was the strange feature protruding from its front cover.

It appeared to be an *eye*.

The eye was shut tight, hidden behind a veiny lid. It even had *eyelashes*. The details were all so eerily realistic that on closer inspection, Emrys thought the leather binding of the book— warm to the touch and strangely supple—well, it could almost be . . . skin.

The book was like a living thing. Alive and fragile . . . and asleep.

Emrys drew a shaky breath. He tried to fight against the tremor in his arms. "What . . . the . . ."

"Open it," Hazel whispered.

"I don't know, you guys," said Serena, looking properly spooked for once. "That thing looks . . . it feels . . . does . . . does anyone else feel that?"

"I'm going to put it back," said Emrys, and his hands shook more severely than ever. "I'll . . . I'll just—"

At that moment, the book seemed to shudder.

The eye set within its cover wrenched open.

It looked right at them.

It *saw* them.

Then Emrys felt a pain so intense, it left him no breath with which to scream.

The Doomsday Archives

From the New Rotterdam Wiki Project

⭐ *This article is a _stub_. You can help by _expanding it_.*

> To meet our site's quality standards, this article may require cleanup.

> This article may require copy editing for grammar, style, cohesion, or tone. You can assist by _editing it_.

The Doomsday Archives is the hidden place in New Rotterdam where all the weird stuff that happens here gets cataloged. [*citation needed*] Strange figures have appeared around town, at the sites of hauntings or unexplained deaths, and they always leave with an object from the scene. [*citation needed*] They might even be the cause of all these problems, like the Illuminati. [*speculation?*] Sometimes witnesses try to follow them, but the strangers always disappear before anyone can find out where they go.

Watch the doors. [*clarification needed*]

5

The pain was like a flower: a bud that unfolded, petal by petal, into an exquisite blossom of agony. It swelled just behind Emrys's right eye. He scratched at his face, howling wordlessly, and heard his friends doing much the same.

But Emrys had little consideration to spare for Hazel or Serena. His own torment was so demanding that he could think of nothing else. If his eye wasn't already squeezed shut, he might have clawed it out just to end this suffering. Whatever living ember had somehow burrowed into his face was sharp and hot, angry and wriggling.

And then, miraculously . . . it was gone.

Just as quickly as it had come, the pain dulled. The chorus of wails that had surrounded Emrys quieted into low, shocked whimpers.

He heard his own breath coming out as a wheezing percussion. Beside him, Hazel moaned, and Serena let out a sob. Emrys blinked against his tears, saw the fuzzy shapes of the others. They were both clutching their right eyes.

"What . . . ?" Hazel asked thickly. "What was *that*?"

"Dad!" Serena bawled. "I want my dads!"

Emrys thought she might very well get her wish. The whole building must have heard them shrieking bloody murder from the open penthouse apartment. Emrys's own throat was raw from screaming. Any moment now, his parents would burst upward, finding the three kids groaning and crying.

"You guys . . . where *are* we?"

The shock in Hazel's voice drew Emrys from his thoughts. He wiped furiously at his eyes, focusing his vision on the ransacked penthouse. Only—it wasn't.

The room that surrounded them was massive—far bigger than even Van Stavern's spacious loft apartment. The ceiling stretched upward in a series of decorative arches, culminating dozens of feet from the floor.

And speaking of the floor, Emrys realized that the surface pressing painfully into his hip was neither the ancient vinyl flooring shared by most of the apartments in the building, nor the planks Van Stavern had covered his loft with. Instead, marble tiles stretched from wall to wall, polished and gleaming. The stone was cool against his palm.

He pushed himself up, standing shakily, as did Serena and Hazel. Somehow, impossibly, the world had shifted around Emrys and his friends, depositing them from Van Stavern's apartment into this new place.

"No," Serena said. "No, this isn't real. This is a dream."

"There are so many *books*," Hazel noted with awe.

The walls were covered in them, in fact. Far more even than in Van Stavern's apartment. Shelves that were three times as tall as Emrys climbed the edges of the chamber, each laden with heavy tomes. Some of the books looked ancient, their leather bindings brittle and peeling. Others were clearly new, with spines wrapped in colorful paper and stamped with foil titles.

But strangest by far were the displays. All around the room—set artfully across plinths, cabinets, and in gleaming glass cases—was a gallery of curios straight out of a horror movie. There were grinning masks and vacant-eyed dolls. A dagger's curved blade seemed to drip with dark ichor when Emrys saw it from the corner of his eye, but was clean and polished when he glanced directly at it. In one display, an iron lantern housed a single bulbous candle, the wax of which had melted into a configuration that looked startlingly like a screaming face.

The chamber also contained chairs, sofas, and sumptuous carpets, all arranged around what appeared to be a functional fireplace. Skulls of various alarming shapes and sizes lined the mantel above it. There were doors, too, half a dozen of them leading who-knew-where, though they were all dwarfed by what Emrys could only think of as the *main* door—a colossal spire of dark wood that crested into several menacing points. Its antique knob was cast in bronze—except for the blue-and-white enamel eye at its center.

Serena stepped up to a standing mirror. It was a flat pane of silver, wreathed by sharp metal leaves. The mirror reflected the room back at her, but with one important difference.

"Whoa . . ." she breathed.

Serena wasn't in it.

"What is this place?" Emrys asked, moving beside her. He, too, cast no reflection. He waved a hand over the surface of the mirror, where no one waved back.

Emrys glanced to Hazel, who gave him a wide grin; he felt himself beaming back at her.

It was real. All of it. The ghost stories and urban legends they'd been chasing since camp, cataloging every haunted bread crumb, were *real*. And had led them *here*. It was as if this gallery of haunted objects had been made just for them.

This place—this eerie, improbable place—was *theirs*.

Emrys approached a nearby plinth, on which a small dried hand was laid beneath a glass bell jar. As he got closer, he realized it was actually a paw—a monkey's paw—with four tiny digits curled into the palm and one outstretched. Emrys reached toward the glass, his own fingers fluttering.

"I wouldn't touch that if I were you," a new voice intoned. It was steady and aged, the voice of a grown-up. "You'll find it's terrifically cursed."

Emrys yelped. He spun around, searching for the stranger. But all he saw were his friends.

"Down here," the voice said.

Emrys looked to where the strange book lay on the marble floor, abandoned in all the excitement. The eye at the center was still open. It turned in its leathery socket, settling on Emrys.

"So you've found the reliquary," the voice said, echoing from the tome. "Then I suppose it can't be helped. Welcome to the Order of the Azure Eye."

The room was deathly silent as Emrys and his friends stared at the talking book.

"Did anyone else hear that?" Emrys asked in a high, nervous voice. "*Please* tell me someone else heard that."

"S-speakers . . ." Serena declared weakly. "Speakers in the floor."

"One speaker, actually," the book said. "In the Atlas. My name is Alyx Van Stavern. I live in apartment #701. And you, I take it, must be the children from the lower floors—the ones who have been spying on me."

Emrys let out a little gasp. Van Stavern had known they were watching him?

"*You're* Van Stavern?" Hazel asked. She crouched to get a better look at the book, which swiveled its blue eye toward her. "What happened to you? Your apartment's been destroyed."

A weary sigh emanated from the tome, as clearly as if the man were standing right there.

"I should start at the beginning," it muttered. "Or as close as I can get to it. I'm a member of an organization of . . . well, I suppose you'd call us occult investigators. We are scholars and mystics, adventurers and legionnaires. We come from diverse disciplines and nationalities, each bringing our expertise to a common, crucial aim: protecting our world from the dark forces that threaten it. Or at least we did. As far as I can tell, I'm the last remaining member of the Order. Until today."

"You really *are* a sorcerer," Emrys said.

"One of the best," Van Stavern puffed. "Or I was. But like my fellow members, I was being hunted. An assassin tracked us down, murdering my friends and colleagues one by one. And tonight, cloaked in the storm, that killer finally found me."

"The Whistler . . ." Hazel supplied.

"We heard them coming up the stairs," Emrys said gravely. "I'm sorry, we . . . we didn't know."

"No, you couldn't have," Van Stavern's voice said sadly. "And if you *had* interfered, you'd be dead. This 'Whistler,' as you call them, is part of a very dangerous organization. By the time I sensed the threat, it was already at my doorstep. In my desperation, I cast a rash but fruitful spell, fleeing into the pages of this grimoire. It is the *Atlas of the End*: a spell book, index, and my Order's guiding text. Now, I appear to be . . . stuck."

"Stuck?" Hazel repeated, squinting at the book. "Like, you're possessing it? But where's your body?"

"Weren't you listening?" Van Stavern snapped. "I'm in *here*. *All* of me. And if there's a way to extricate myself, then even I haven't discovered it. Yet."

"This is not happening," Serena said. "You all realize this is impossible, right?"

"It *is* happening," Van Stavern answered darkly. "And your disbelief will not protect you from the powers at work. You're a part of this now—all of you."

"Are you saying we're in danger?" Hazel asked.

Van Stavern sighed again, a weary sound that rang a bit sadly to Emrys. "I wish I could tell you *no*," the book said. "But living in New Rotterdam, you must have guessed by now that danger always lurks close at hand. The young are especially vulnerable."

The eyelid at the center of the book hooded thoughtfully. "Beside our world there are . . . other places. Dimensions so unlike our own that they contort the very laws of nature where they press close, defying physics and biology. And there are places where the barriers that separate us from these forces are especially delicate. Places like New Rotterdam. Very ancient, very *powerful* beings are pushing against the other side of the door, hoping to break into your town. To call them monsters is an understatement. These are the gods monsters worship."

The eye rose, gazing at each of the three in turn. When it settled on him, Emrys felt the hairs rising along his arms.

"The proximity of these beings means that tendrils of their influence can leak into our world, imbuing even mundane items with supernatural qualities. These objects become what the Order calls *relics*. On their own, the relics are dangerous enough, but it's in the hands of *people* that they become truly potent—and potentially catastrophic. And so, the Order of the Azure Eye was created to hunt the relics down, keeping them safely contained within this reliquary."

"The Doomsday Archives . . ." Emrys breathed.

"The *what?*" Serena asked, at the same moment the Atlas said, "*Pardon* me?"

"It's an article from the New Rotterdam Wiki," Emrys continued. "One of the oldest, actually. Every year, some new admin threatens to delete it, because there's not a shred of evidence to back it up. But it always survives. No one knows who the original author was, but they claimed mysterious figures sometimes appear around the sites where weird stuff happens in town. Supposedly these figures take objects from the sites and disappear. It's the name they gave you—or gave this place."

"Not entirely inaccurate," Van Stavern murmured thoughtfully. "Any number of relics could result in a doomsday scenario if left in the wrong hands. But it's possible that this *wiki*"—Van Stavern pronounced the word like *we key*—"refers to the group who sent my rather musical assassin after me. They are a dark counterpart to the Order: the Yellow Court."

Emrys frowned. He tried to remember if he'd ever encountered *that* name on the wiki, but nothing sprang to mind. It was amazing how even the combined knowledge of hundreds amounted to so little.

"Who are they?" he asked. "Another secret society? The cult of an evil god? Ooh—are they relic hunters, too?"

"Who they are . . . is hard to say at the moment," Van Stavern admitted, the eye lowering. "The Court have been frustratingly adept at hiding their aims and identities. What I *can* tell you is that they're ruthless, they're insidious, and they appear to have a sizable collection of their own, yes. But rather than just hunting relics, the Court often sets them out in the open, exactly where they're likely to do the most damage. We've tied dozens of supernatural disasters to their activities."

"Like what?"

The eye widened. "Haunted dolls are a favorite. Can't tell you why so many dolls end up as relics. A few cursed puzzle boxes. . . . Oh, several years ago we encountered a relic that's a kind of murderous *poem*. No containing that one, I'm afraid."

"No way!" Emrys gasped. "The Laughing Man is real?"

"That's the one! And yes, so I'd avoid reading it aloud after dark. Nasty bit of work. The Yellow Court was responsible for the poem being published widely."

"It almost sounds like the Yellow Court is conducting experiments," Hazel said thoughtfully. "Watching how people use the relics—or how the relics use them."

"An interesting—and disturbing—idea," the book muttered. "But whatever their goals, as the newest members of the Order of the Azure Eye, it is *your* duty to oppose them."

"Like, fight them?" Hazel asked. "How? We're not wizards or monster hunters. We're just kids."

"I'm not *fighting* anyone!" Serena cried. "Certainly not on the word of some creepy talking book. How do we know anything he's saying is even true?"

"Serena, how can you deny what's happening?" Emrys waved his arms wildly. "We're standing in a room that couldn't fit into our whole *building*, much less a single apartment. This *is* real! And so are the bad things hurting people in New Rotterdam."

"That's exactly the problem," Serena shot back. "I get it, we like horror—*movies*. Urban legends. Fiction. The whole point is getting scared in a way that's safe. But this is really, truly dangerous! Even *he* said so!" She pointed toward the Atlas on the floor. "Who knows if that Whistler is coming back?"

Emrys felt himself vibrating with frustration. Serena was the most fearless person he knew, and *now* she was balking? Hadn't she just been scoffing at the very idea of living in fear? Emrys was the anxious one of the group—the downer. But now that they were on the precipice of something incredible, it was like they'd switched places.

"The danger is already here!" he said. "It's just that nobody wants to look at it! We're being given the chance to do more than sit around worrying about the world, waiting for grown-ups to care."

Serena groaned. "How do we know that's really Alyx Van Stavern in there? We aren't even sure he's one of the good guys!" Her expression softened a touch. "I get why you want this, Emrys. I do. But there's so much we don't know yet. We need to *think* before we agree to be a part of some supernatural war."

Emrys glanced pleadingly to Hazel, hoping she'd back him up.

But his friend hesitated, biting her lip.

Emrys's heart skipped a beat. While it was true that he and Hazel had been close for years, she and Serena had history, too—history that he wasn't a part of. *Emrys* was the newcomer: to New Rotterdam, to their building, and to this strange, teetering friendship triangle. Where Hazel and Emrys connected through shared passions, Serena called to Hazel's sense of logic. He honestly couldn't tell which was winning.

But then Hazel's mouth stretched into a thin, determined line. "I'm with Emrys," she said. "Now that we're here—how can we turn back?"

"You can't," Van Stavern's voice sounded from the book. "What is seen cannot be unseen. The Atlas has *already* chosen you." The blue orb at the center of the Atlas narrowed. "You've all been marked by the Azure Eye."

The Laughing Man

From the New Rotterdam Wiki Project

The Laughing Man refers both to a popular children's poem and the figure described by the poem itself. First printed in the New Rotterdam Watcher in 1973, "The Laughing Man" was submitted to the paper's first (and only) Children's Poetry Contest by eleven-year-old Cecilia Pike.

> *Grinning 'neath the moonlit sky,*
> *the laughing man has caught your eye.*
> *Dancing, racing, writhing game!*
> *He's seen your face. He knows your name!*
> *Laughing. Screaming! Whooping cheer.*
> *The laughing man rings in your ear.*
> *Gaining. Almost. Nearly there!*
> *He's close enough to grab your hair.*
> *Fingers reaching, footfalls spry.*
> *If he gets you, then you will*

While most initially believed the missing word was the result of a printing error, the paper eventually revealed that it was a purposeful omission on the part of the young author, "inviting readers to supply the ending of their choice." Even so, the Watcher received numerous complaints about the poem's strangely menacing tone. It wasn't long before rumors began circulating that the rhyme itself was cursed, and anyone who finished it—inserting the logical final word at the poem's conclusion [1]—would be butchered by the Laughing Man.

Indeed, the summer of 1973 saw a rash of grisly murders. While most of the killings were eventually attributed to serial killer Jack Allen Casey, a number contained conflicting details that cast doubt on his involvement. "The Laughing Man" quickly entered the public imagination as an enduring local taboo.

In 2008, reporter Emily Hatcher-Thorn began planning a piece commemorating "The Laughing Man" for the Watcher and hoped to interview its author, Cecilia Pike, who would have been forty-five at the time. Instead, Hatcher-Thorn discovered that the only New Rotterdam resident to bear that name had died a hundred years prior to the poem's printing, murdered on the night of June 7, 1873. Cecilia was eleven years old at the time. Days after posting her discovery on social media, Hatcher-Thorn herself went missing. Her whereabouts are still unknown.

Notes

1. **Editorial note.** As many of our administrators are New Rotterdam residents with strong feelings about the subject, official policy is that the poem's final word will *never* be included in the body of this article. For this reason, editing privileges are locked.

6

"Marked?" Emrys asked. "What do you mean?"

He began searching his arms and legs for cursed symbols or mysterious new tattoos. His parents would kill him if he showed up to breakfast with fresh ink.

The Atlas didn't have an eyebrow, but if it did, Emrys imagined it would be quirked at him right then. It gazed at him with a look of potent exasperation. "That pain you felt earlier was the first gift of our Order. Consider it a kind of second sight. From this point on, you'll all receive glimpses of the truth beyond the fiction. You'll sense the otherworldly, though your abilities will be hazy at first.

"Unfortunately, this gift is a double-edged sword," Van Stavern continued. "The invisible world doesn't like being seen, I'm afraid. Like a spider's web, it has a way of ensnaring those who brush against it. Your best chance for survival is going through with this. Now—would one of you be kind enough to pick me up off the floor?"

Emrys lifted the book, holding it out from his chest. He could feel the eye's jerky movements in his palms, even through the tome's thick pages and leather binding. He did his best to swallow his discomfort.

"But you are not defenseless," Van Stavern said. "The three of you stand amongst the greatest collection of occult relics in the known world. For centuries, the Blue Reliquary has functioned as a sanctuary, a war room, and occasionally a cost-free event space. But its true purpose is to contain *relics*—items imbued with uncanny abilities. Some are famous, others obscure, but each is uniquely powerful, as well as uniquely dangerous."

"Would we have heard of any of them?" Emrys asked.

"That depends on your knowledge of history and mythology," the book said. "Our Order has collected everything from the Wings of Icarus to the Staff of the Monkey King. And, again, there's the haunted doll room, if that's your thing. Agree to join our esteemed ranks, and each of you may select a relic from the Order's collection as a personal requisition. But only one, mind you. Mixing arcane forces can tend to have unpredictable results."

Emrys's eyes widened. He glanced around the space, which was *packed* with haunted relics. He could actually take one of them with him? To *keep*?

"What do they do?" Hazel asked in a hushed voice. "How do we know which ones to take?"

All three kids peered at the many strange and wonderful objects on display. Even Serena.

"I can provide background on particular items," Van Stavern said, "but choosing is as much about intuition as information. A relic will resonate with a suitable bearer. As simplistic as it sounds, I suggest you go with your gut."

"Won't some of these be a bit . . . noticeable?" Serena asked, eying a gargantuan hammer covered in Norse runes.

"The Order has ways of disguising our personal relics. You don't last this long as a secret society by brandishing Excalibur on every street corner."

Excalibur? Emrys guessed Van Stavern was joking. . . . Probably.

"What's this one?" Hazel asked. She approached a plinth, on which rested an intricate metal diadem. At the front of the circlet, silvery cords had been shaped into a set of interlocking shapes—a triangle contained a square, which enclosed a circle. And set in the center of this final loop was a tiny, vivid-red stone.

Unlike the clean, polished metal of the circlet itself, the gem was rough and uncut. It glittered strangely in the light of the reliquary.

"The Magnus Crown," Van Stavern said. "Containing the fabled philosopher's stone. First discovered by Albertus Magnus in the thirteenth century, the Order had it set into this circlet for ease of use sometime in the seventeenth. Not to worry—it's quite sturdy. There's no risk of the stone shaking loose."

Hazel's mouth dropped. "Wait, you mean, like, alchemy? The philosopher's stone that lets people turn lead into *gold*?"

"In the hands of an acquisitive wielder, certainly," the book answered. "But it can do so much more than generate riches. The crown's bearer can stitch and sunder *any* molecular bonds, transmuting elements and compounds. You could rust an iron cell to ash or make a glass of water explode. Many of the applications involve exploding, actually. There are limits, of course. Energy is neither created nor destroyed, so the wielder must sacrifice their own metabolism to fuel larger reactions. Oh, and I wouldn't get any ideas about trying it on living creatures. The results are . . . disturbing."

"I can't believe it," Hazel said. "I'm really looking at *the* philosopher's stone?"

"As I said, the powers at your disposal are considerable," Van Stavern intoned. "But mastery won't come easily. It may take months or even years to unlock just a fraction of their potential."

Hazel bit her lip, then gently lifted the crown from the plinth. With a small exhalation, she settled the circlet down on her own head. "Who's next?" she asked.

Emrys's thoughts churned. He watched Serena as she stepped hesitantly toward a shield, peering into its silvery surface.

Hazel approached him. "Do you want to look around a bit?" she asked.

Emrys shook his head. "I already know which relic I'm going to pick," he said.

Hazel's face clouded with confusion. Then Emrys held up the Atlas.

"Really?" she asked. "Is that even possible?"

Emrys turned the tome over in his hands. "You're a spell book, right?" he said. "Well, teach me magic."

The eye on the book's cover rolled in his direction, watching Emrys for a long beat.

"I am not a book," Van Stavern finally said. "But I will teach you. The *Atlas of the End* is yours—for now—with one small warning. Sorcery is not for the squeamish, Emrys. Many great witches and wizards have served the Order and contributed to this text: Merlin, Ursula Southeil, Marie Laveau. Many more have failed where they succeeded. You must be sure."

Was he? For a moment, Emrys faltered. Perhaps a more straightforward relic would be better for fighting monsters. There were any number of razor-sharp swords lining the gallery walls.

But somehow Emrys knew that wasn't his path. Van Stavern had said the Atlas was his Order's *guiding text*. It was like their version of the wiki. Emrys wasn't completely sure what he'd find inside, but the mysteries called to him.

And Serena had been right about one thing: he *did* want this. It was scary, sure. The secrets Emrys had been chasing his whole life had finally found *him*, and he was enough of a horror fan to know how badly that could go. But if Emrys could learn to harness the powers at work here—rather than fall victim to them—maybe he'd have a real chance at fixing some of what was wrong with the world.

Emrys's parents had always told him: all it would take was the right book to unlock a passion for reading. He suspected he'd finally found it.

"I'm sure," he said firmly.

Which brought them to Serena. In all the time they'd been talking, the girl had barely moved from the gleaming shield. Serena watched it with an almost hypnotic fascination.

"The Aegis of Truth," Van Stavern said softly, breaking Serena out of her reverie. She blinked, glancing toward Emrys and Hazel.

"It's one of the oldest and most famous relics we have," Van Stavern said. "No doubt you've heard the tale. Medusa, the snake-haired gorgon. Perseus, the hero who avoided her petrifying gaze. The Aegis is a *powerful* relic, capable of reflecting occult powers. Perhaps even more devastating, its mirrored surface reveals *truth*, which can be a grimmer foe than any monster."

The eye swiveled in its socket, turning from shield to girl. "It's calling to you, isn't it? The shield chooses those with stout hearts and keen minds. Heroes. Truth-seekers."

For the first time Emrys could remember, Serena seemed genuinely awestruck. Her eyes were wide with wonderment. And in that moment, the sense of destiny that Emrys had been feeling—that they were meant to be here; all three of them, together—rose, along with every hair on his neck.

This was real.

They were going to save the—

"No."

Serena took a step back from the shield, her face pulling into a scowl. "It's too much, too fast," she said. "I'm not joining some battle against evil knickknacks on a whim. You two do what you want. I won't snitch, but I won't be forced into it, either."

The girl turned her withering gaze on Emrys . . . and the book nestled in his arms.

"Now listen closely, Professor Hex, because I don't like repeating myself. Take. Me. Home."

INTERLUDE

Casper Leonard loved storms.

The bigger, the better, as far as he was concerned. He loved the way they reminded humanity of its smallness. He took a strange comfort in knowing that the responsibilities on his ever-growing list were fleeting, in the grand scheme of things. That all our pressing little tasks—our bustling cities and profound works of art—amounted to little more than a layer of dust to be scrubbed clean by nature's sweeping hand.

And tonight's pressing little task was laundry.

Casper had been so busy studying for his upcoming exam that he'd failed to notice the dwindling pile of clean underwear until it was too late. Now, with the World History test tomorrow and the storm raging overhead, he'd found himself without anything to wear to the exam.

Just as his parents had promised, life as a freshman at Acheron University had been a time of awakenings for Casper, though most of them were of the *rude* variety. He'd had chores back home, of course, but not quite so many of them, and not all at the same time.

Thankfully, the Screamin' Suds twenty-four-hour laundromat stayed open through the storm, though its owner, Mr. Landon, had yet to emerge from the back. Casper was alone, except for the faded poster of Infra Red, Mr. Landon's favorite singer, her head curled back in what looked like an epic shriek.

Casper didn't mind the solitude. He reclined in a plastic seat, reading and re-reading the same paragraph about Marco Polo's meeting with Kublai Khan. Outside, wind pummeled the laundromat's windows with shadowy fists. Occasionally, strobes of lightning brightened the sky, startling Casper like sudden headlights.

He just hoped the power stayed on long enough for the rinse cycle to finish. He could air-dry his boxers if it came to it.

As if on cue, the fluorescent lights flickered overhead. Casper sucked in a breath, waiting for darkness to fall over him like a blanket. But the power held. The world kept spinning, and the washing machine with it. Propped against Casper's chest, Marco Polo kneeled before Kublai Khan, their pivotal meeting suspended in time.

Casper only caught sight of the hourglass because of the lightning.

A glittering lance of brilliance illuminated the street outside—and there it was, propped against the curb. Its elegant, golden frame was shocking enough to see in a place like this, but Casper swore the sand inside the top bulb looked dark and pulpy. Almost . . . red.

As the brightness faded, the street was plunged into shadow again. A moment later, thunder growled.

Casper stood, setting his textbook aside. He stalked toward the window, gazing out into the blustery gloom, and waited for another flicker in the sky.

He didn't need to wait long. A bright flash of lightning spotlighted the hourglass. The sand was definitely red. Bizarre. As Casper watched, grains began to snake down into the lower bulb, as if some inner timer had just been activated. The sand was hypnotic to watch, curling lazily downward into a small but expanding pile.

The silence struck him like a blow. All the noise of the laundromat just vanished—the creak of the washing machine and rattle of wind replaced by a riotous quiet. Casper's arms exploded with goose bumps. At first, he thought the power must have finally gone out, but that wasn't right. The lights were still on. And outside . . .

He gasped as he looked out the window. A silvery fork of lightning still stretched across the sky, skewering clouds like they were oozing hunks of meat. It just hung there, frozen in place.

"That's not possible," Casper mumbled, the words ridiculous even to his own ears. That wasn't how lightning worked. This wasn't how the *world* worked. And yet . . .

He pushed against the door handle and it swung open easily. Outside, the street was just as silent as the laundromat. Rain was suspended in the air, tiny needles of moisture that melted at his touch, dampening his skin. Casper listened for cars navigating the wet roads, or wind buffeting the trees. Nothing.

Until he saw the figure.

An old woman stood in the middle of the road, her creamy cardigan and velvet slippers jarringly inappropriate for the weather. She didn't even have an umbrella! But she smiled at Casper. Her eyes were vague, almost lethargic.

Though the sight of the woman was unnerving, Casper raised his hand in greeting. Had she wandered away from an assisted-living facility somewhere? Maybe she was in trouble.

The woman raised her hand back.

"Hello?" he called.

"Hello, Casper," she said. "My, this storm is something, isn't it? They say bad weather always looks worse through a window, but it's plenty vicious out here." She tilted her head. "Could you do me a favor, dear?"

Casper took a step forward, squinting at the stranger.

"I'm sorry, do I know you?" She didn't *look* familiar. And where would he even have encountered her? Casper had only lived in New Rotterdam since the start of the semester. Could this strange old lady possibly be from the university?

The woman's smile widened. Her hazy eyes focused. "Normally, I wouldn't rush things," she said, ignoring his question. "You all have so little time as it is. But this weather has me

feeling sluggish. Do you mind if we skip the chase entirely? Just this once."

"The . . . chase?" Casper repeated. He didn't like this.

He glanced nervously toward the laundromat. The door was still open. How quickly could he get inside and bar the entrance if he had to? Casper turned back and—

The face that now hovered inches from his own did not belong to an old woman. Skin peeled back into leathery folds, unveiling a cavern of a mouth that was lined with horrific, barbed teeth. The face dangled in midair from a sinewy throat— a throat that was quickly swelling open with each throb of serpentine muscle.

Casper screamed. The fangs closed down.

The street went quiet again.

From several feet away, an hourglass counted patiently, the lone witness to Casper's fate. He disappeared that night, scrubbed clean from the world beneath the silent storm.

7

When Emrys awoke the next morning, the Atlas was gone.

He sprung up from his bed in a panic. He didn't believe for a second that it had all been a dream—no dream could be so vivid. But he'd left the Atlas at his bedside, within easy reach and his immediate line of sight, just as he had when Sir Galahound had been a frightened little puppy in a brand-new home.

He might be an initiate of the Order of the Azure Eye—*marked* in some intangible way—but that book was Emrys's sole physical connection to a world of myths and monsters. It was *proof*—not only that the unseen world existed, but that Emrys had a place there. Besides that, the Atlas was a living being in Emrys's care. Had he failed his charge already? Had his mom found the book while he'd been sleeping? Or his dog? Or the— what were they called—the Yellow Court? Could they have tracked him down so soon?

In his groggy panic, Emrys took a few moments to realize the Atlas had been replaced by a notebook he'd never seen before.

It appeared to be a standard composition book, with black binding, rounded edges, and a black-and-white speckled cover. It was gently used and thoroughly unremarkable—with the exception of a drawing, scrawled in blue ink, set right in the center of the notebook's front cover.

It was a drawing of an eye.

"No way," said Emrys, and, feeling only a little silly, he poked the notebook. "Uh, Mr. Van Stavern? Is that . . . is that you?"

The simple blue sketch bulged outward, like glass warping beneath a flame. A second later, Van Stavern's uncanny eye was blinking, its pupil shrinking in the early morning light. The narrow spine expanded, and the cardstock cover rippled, seeming to sag before snapping into shape, taut and leathery.

"Hm?" said Van Stavern. "What is it? You look as if you've just seen an eldritch evocation."

"I didn't recognize you," said Emrys. Of course, Van Stavern had mentioned the relics could disguise themselves, and the Atlas itself was clearly no exception. It was a convincing facade; no one would suspect a worn-edged composition journal of being a sentient spell book. "Were you . . . sleeping?" asked Emrys.

"Not as such," said Van Stavern. "Just resting my eyes. *Eye.* But I'm glad you're up early. We should take advantage of this respite, before the Yellow Court realizes that the Order isn't quite as extinct as they believe. There's much to teach you, and—I'm sorry, am I boring you?"

"Sorry, sorry," Emrys said through a yawn. He wiped some spittle from the corner of his mouth. "I'm excited to learn more, honest. But my dad's gonna knock on that door any minute and tell me to get ready to leave."

"Leave?" said Van Stavern. "What do you have to do that's more important than this?"

Emrys gave the book a wilting look. "Dude, it's a Friday. What do you think? I've gotta go to school." He opened his backpack. "And you're coming with."

In the end, Emrys opted to put the Atlas in a rarely used tote bag. The inside of his backpack was a mess of pencil shavings, old handouts, and candy wrappers. It wouldn't have felt right shoving Van Stavern in there, wedged between well-worn textbooks.

He tried to keep a steady gait as he walked to school beside Hazel, determined to keep his hip from banging against Van Stavern with each step. He felt a momentary pang of jealousy; *her* relic had taken the form of an unobtrusive headband. It fit her perfectly and seemed downright fashionable, as far as Emrys could tell.

It seemed to Emrys that they should have a million things to talk about, but somehow, their walk was quieter than it had ever been. Emrys had the strangest feeling that everything that had happened the night before was just so *tentative*. Like a web of delicate gossamer, invisible unless you saw it at just the right angle, and no less fragile or impermanent once you knew it was there. Breathe on it wrong, and all that beautiful latticework was just ribbons on the wind.

"Have you heard from Serena?" he asked her. She shook her head.

"She's not really a morning person," Hazel said. "I'm sure we'll talk tonight."

"I hope she's okay," said Emrys, but he wasn't even sure what he meant. Okay that their whole world had turned inside out? Fine with the idea that her best friend and the new kid had joined a club she wanted nothing to do with? Safe from the Yellow Court and whatever dark forces they revered?

Serena hadn't seemed okay by any measure when they'd seen her last. At her insistence, Van Stavern had sent the three home the previous night, uttering a muffled incantation before the reliquary's enormous, spired doorway. To their shock, the door opened back into Van Stavern's trashed apartment. Once they'd passed through, it closed swiftly behind them.

Swiveling around, however, Emrys had found only a closed broom closet. Inside was an ancient vacuum cleaner and little else. Serena cursed the vacuum cleaner, gestured rudely at the Atlas, gave Hazel a perfunctory hug, and pointedly ignored Emrys as she'd stormed downstairs ahead of them.

He knew he wouldn't see her at school. Serena went to a private school, the Academy of the Sacred Silence, which sat up on a hill, beyond the reach of the morning mist that clutched at Emrys's and Hazel's ankles as if seeking to trip them. Emrys had seen the Academy once, through a gap in the well-kept hedges that served as its border. It had a fountain!

Emrys and Hazel, on the other hand, attended Gideon de Ruiter Middle School, which sat at the city's lowest point, so that the ever-present mist rolled downhill to gather around the school like smoke from a witch's cauldron. The sign out front, a great stone slab bearing the school's name and motto, resembled nothing so much as a great tombstone, and a rusty, sharp-edged metal fence enclosed the campus. The school looked altogether less like a seat of learning and more like a cemetery.

"You're fidgeting," said a voice, and Emrys snapped out of his reverie. He had momentarily forgotten Van Stavern was there.

"Weird," said Hazel. "It's like literally having an angel on your shoulder."

Emrys *had* been fidgeting, tugging on the tote's straps, which would have made it a bumpy ride for Van Stavern, despite his best intentions. He realized now that his anxiety had been quietly building all morning. His heart was racing, and his mouth was dry.

This was more than the usual school-morning jitters. The whole world had been flipped on its head last night. As the exhilaration wore off, the doubt crept in.

Secret societies. Cursed relics. Emrys had been vindicated for every uncanny belief he'd ever held.

But it all came with an unexpected edge. The Yellow Court. The whistling assassin. Other-dimensional beings trying to poke holes into the world? Emrys had already been plenty worried about the state of the world *before* all that.

Hazel instinctively touched the stone sign as she passed onto school grounds, and Emrys followed suit. The granite felt almost silky, worn smooth by the elements—and by the touch of thousands of hands over the years. As legend had it, the last sixth grader to pass the front entrance without touching the school sign had been cursed with spectacularly bad luck. No one seemed to agree on what exactly had befallen the student—in his short time at the school, Emrys had heard everything from "failed every pop quiz for a year" to "crushed by the retractable bleachers"—but the entire sixth grade seemed to make it a point to touch the entry stone each morning.

Emrys didn't believe *every* superstition was true. But he also believed in being safe over being sorry. What could it hurt to touch the stone every day?

As long as he remembered to wash his hands.

"Look," Hazel said, and Emrys saw immediately what she'd noticed. There was a police cruiser parked out front, in the lane reserved for buses. Two police officers stood beside the entrance—if not for the cruiser, Emrys would have missed them entirely, because they weren't in uniform. They wore dark suits, their badges clipped to their belts and their guns hidden from sight. But Emrys could see the holster straps beneath their suit jackets.

Guns did not put him at ease.

"What?" said Van Stavern. "Why have you stopped?"

"The police are here," answered Hazel. "They look like detectives. They're talking to the guidance counselor."

"Do you think they found your apartment?" asked Emrys. His heart beat faster. "Do you think they're here for *us*?"

"Absolutely not," said Van Stavern. "I told you, there were . . . *contingencies* in place. No one will come looking for me." The spell book chuckled. "If the police came sniffing around every time a member of the Order went missing under mysterious circumstances, we'd have been exposed eons ago."

Hazel scowled. "Is that supposed to make us feel better?" she asked. "We're in the Order now."

Van Stavern sniffed. "I'm sure you'll do *fine*," he said. "You have me to guide you. Just act natural. You aren't guilty of anything, after all."

Emrys tried to take the sorcerer's words to heart. But he couldn't help thinking how they'd left their fingerprints all over Van Stavern's apartment. Emrys had ripped a hole in the floor! What had he been thinking?

Back in his room, Emrys had plied Van Stavern for details about what had happened late into the night, but Van Stavern had a gift for vague answers and cryptic mutterings that discouraged continued questioning. The interaction had done little to put Emrys's fears to rest.

As they passed the detectives, Emrys's palms began to sweat. He suddenly remembered every time he'd ever broken a rule in his entire life. And the spell book on his shoulder (technically stolen while trespassing in a crime scene, he remembered) felt conspicuous and heavy. He fiddled with the strap unconsciously.

One of the detectives—a tall, reedy man with sallow skin—looked up from his notepad as they passed. Emrys could feel the man's eyes on him, but he resisted the urge to look back. He willed himself to act natural. Whatever *that* looked like.

When they'd crossed the threshold into the school, he finally risked a look over his shoulder. The detective was writing something in his notebook. He didn't seem to have noticed Emrys at all.

Their first-period teacher, Ms. Joanna, opened the school day with an announcement. "A student has gone missing," she said. "An eighth grader, Brian Skupp. He was last seen on school grounds earlier this week. The police believe that he ran away."

That explained the detectives. Emrys felt a momentary rush of relief—they weren't there for *him*—then a stab of guilt for thinking of himself first. He looked across the aisle to Hazel, who appeared somber, but not especially troubled. The name didn't seem to mean any more to her than it did to him.

"If you have any information, please speak to the school's student success coordinator, Mr. Maple—or any adult." Ms. Joanna smiled, her pale white face beaming. Ms. Joanna was always smiling, even when it was inappropriate—as was often the case when discussing American history. It seemed calculated to put her students at ease, but it often had the opposite effect on Emrys. "And Mr. Maple has asked me to remind you that his door remains open should you experience any *negative emotions* or feel otherwise triggered as a result of this situation. Now, if you'll open your textbooks to page eighty-two . . ."

Emrys felt a disorienting sense of vertigo, as he did whenever he was pulled from a macabre or weighty subject. He tried to shake it off—willed himself not to spiral over thoughts of Brian Skupp or the Yellow Court or whether Van Stavern could breathe okay in that tote bag, if he needed to breathe at all—and as he dug through his backpack for his history textbook, he saw his phone's screen was lit.

Emrys took the phone from his bag and saw he'd missed several texts from Serena. He tried to read them surreptitiously, but he was too slow.

"Emrys! Is that a phone I see?" said the teacher, smiling even as she admonished him. She shook her head as if amused. "I'm afraid I'll have to take that off your hands, young man."

Someone across the room said, "Ooooh, new kid's in trouble," and Hazel grimaced in sympathy while the rest of the class laughed. Emrys's face burned as he looked up at Ms. Joanna, who stood above his desk, hand outstretched.

"Uh, sorry," he said, handing over his phone.

Ms. Joanna only smiled harder. This close, Emrys could see it failed to reach her eyes.

"I can't believe she took my phone," said Emrys. "Now I have to go all the way back to the portables after school."

"If it makes you feel better, she's a more competent discipli-narian than history teacher," Van Stavern told him. "Her grasp of the Civil War seems rudimentary, at best."

"How do you know that? Wait." Emrys gasped. "Were you *there?*"

"Of course not!" snapped Van Stavern. "Just how old do you think I am?"

It was lunch period, and Hazel had decided to visit the media center to brush up on the periodic table. She hadn't managed to tap into her relic's transmutation abilities yet and seemed to think that studying chemistry would help. Emrys confessed he would rather do anything but that, so Van Stavern had suggested Emrys find a private spot where they could speak freely. Emrys had settled on the third-floor boys' room. Nobody used this restroom if they could help it, and those who did avoided the far mirror, which was broken. It had been fixed at least twice, only to immediately break in the same spiderweb pattern. The custodial staff suspected students were to blame. The students had their own suspicions.

"You take me to the nicest places," said Van Stavern, the spell book's disguise abandoned as Emrys lifted it from his tote. "But this will do. With our Order diminished, the Yellow Court is sure to be emboldened—and they weren't exactly meek before. We'd best begin your education here and now."

Emrys's eyes bugged out. "You mean magic?" he said. "Are you going to teach me a *spell?*"

"Of a sort," answered the book. "Most spell work involves specific components and a bit of light math—"

"Aw, math?!" complained Emrys.

"But!" continued Van Stavern. "We'll begin with a simple invocation. Something any initiate in the Order can achieve, whether or not they have any inclination for the profane geometries. Set me down, would you? If you can find a suitable surface . . ."

Emrys balanced the book on the edge of a sink. As he watched, awestruck, the Atlas opened of its own accord. Its pages turned as if caught in a stiff wind, quickly at first, then slowing to a stop, presumably on the page Van Stavern wanted him to see.

"Look here," said the book. "The incantation you'll need is right near the center of the verso page, set apart from the rest of the text."

"Verso?" echoed Emrys.

"The left," said Van Stavern.

"That . . . doesn't even look like it's in English."

"It isn't," the book scoffed. "The forces with which the Order concerns itself are a far sight older than the English language. But you needn't worry, I'll guide you through it. First, set your hands upon the door over there. That's a janitorial closet, correct? You may touch the handle or the door itself; it doesn't matter."

"Like this?" asked Emrys, gripping the door handle.

"Now, repeat after me," said Van Stavern. "*Ostiarius.*"

"*Ostiarius,*" Emrys repeated, and he thought he felt a sudden breeze. He turned to look, careful to keep his hand in place. Aside from the talking book, there was nothing unusual in view. *Just my imagination.*

"*Aperi,*" said the book.

"*Aperi.*" Now Emrys *knew* he felt something, but it was almost impossible to put into words. He felt a sense of . . . opening. Or anticipation. Like he was in the middle of telling a joke, and the universe itself had stopped to listen, holding its breath for the promised punchline.

Van Stavern finished: "*Portam.*"

"*Portam,*" he said, and the strange sensation he'd felt before snapped away. In its wake, he felt a faint buzzing behind his right eye, and gooseflesh all along his arms.

"Go on," said Van Stavern. "Don't lose your nerve *now*. Open the door."

Emrys turned the doorknob and pulled open the door. The closet was gone. In its place was the Blue Reliquary.

"No way," Emrys whispered. He stuck his hand inside, then ventured a single foot over the threshold. "It isn't an illusion?"

"Nothing so tawdry as that," said Van Stavern. "As I told you before, the Blue Reliquary is a sanctuary to the Order—and the Order is *you*. Immediate access to the place can be the difference between life and . . ." Emrys turned to look at the book.

"Well. It's important that you're able to access the reliquary at all times. And that incantation allows you to do just that. Anywhere you find a *door*, you can find an *entrance*."

"Watch the doors," Emrys mumbled, remembering the ominous line at the end of the Doomsday Archives Wiki page. Did *that* have something to do with *this*?

"What's that?" asked Van Stavern.

"Nothing," said Emrys. "It's just, this is totally unreal. Hazel is going to flip!"

"So long as you keep it between the two of you," said Van Stavern. "As you can imagine, this particular incantation lists high among the Order's most sacred secrets. It is meant only for those initiated into our mysteries, and has been jealously guarded over the centuries, a privileged secret shared from one member to the next over the course of—young man, are you *writing the Order's incantatory arcanum onto your arm with a Sharpie?*"

"No!" Emrys said, quickly lowering his marker. "Well, yes. I mean, it's a lot to remember."

"You're the one who wanted to learn 'magic,' as you put it." Van Stavern tutted. "So *learn*."

Emrys shut the door. He expected the dull throb behind his eye to shut with it, but the discomfort persisted. It even grew. "Ow," he said. "Is there—do I need to do something else to end the spell, or . . . ?"

He opened the door again. The Blue Reliquary was gone. In its place was a standard janitorial closet, with paper products and a mop and . . . was that sand?

Red sand, it looked like, pooled on the closet floor like a bloodstain.

"I don't feel so good," said Emrys. He turned to the nearest sink, splashing his face with water. He looked up, intending to get a look at himself in the mirror.

But the mirror was broken. Cracked into jagged shards, like a serrated spider's web.

And the dead-eyed face that looked back at Emrys wasn't his.

The Shadow in the Mirror

From the New Rotterdam Wiki Project

When Gwendoline O'Rear first saw the shadow in the mirror, she thought it a trick of the light. A New Rotterdam teenager in the summer of 1954, she'd been brushing her hair in her powder room, scrutinizing her reflection for the day ahead. As she finished, Gwen stepped away to greet her family, but something made her turn back. There she saw a dark outline in the mirror, right where she'd been standing, as if her reflection had left a residue against the glass. She rubbed her eyes, and the shape disappeared.

"A curious optical illusion," she wrote in her diary later that week. "At least I thought so. Then it kept reappearing." Her diary describes the shadow turning up several more times over the week, and then the weeks to come. Always in her powder room mirror. Each time, it lingered a bit longer, its edges growing sharper. Though Gwen knew she should be disturbed by the apparition, she wrote of a strange fascination with it.

> Such subtle colors shift within its boundaries, like an oil slick catching the light! I find them soothing. They distract me from the dolor of this monotonous life, from my endlessly needful family and the judging

> *gazes of the other girls at school. Today it waved as*
> *I left, as if we were two bosom friends departing.*
> Gwendoline O'Rear's Diary, 1954

According to her family, Gwendoline began spending an increasing amount of time preparing each day, and yet every morning she'd arrive at breakfast looking tired and disheveled. Then Gwen's final entry takes a sudden turn.

> *The shadow tried to grab me by the neck today.*
> *It is no friend. Only now do I see the trap. Its colors*
> *transfix me while it siphons my essence away,*
> *bit by bit. Every day I waver more, while it grows*
> *more solid. I must destroy it tonight.*
> Gwendoline O'Rear's Diary, 1954

In the police report that was filed after her death, Gwen's mother alleged to have witnessed her daughter's last moments. She described finding Gwen perched before the mirror with an iron poker. She claimed a dark shape loomed in the reflection, like a figure reaching through the glass. As Gwen brought the iron bar down, the mirror shattered. So too did Gwendoline O'Rear. The girl turned to her mother, her face a tangle of spidery cracks. Her final words were, "Too late." Then her body splintered to pieces.

8

Emrys wheeled back with a shriek. The face that regarded him from within the shattered mirror was a ruin. It belonged to an older boy whose skin was pale and slick—almost slimy. Two cavernous pits were all that remained of his eyes.

The boy's mouth sagged open. Emrys half expected him to scream, but instead, red sand poured from between his withered lips, gushing outward in a glittering flood. There was so *much* of it. It spilled through the cracks in the mirror, fine grains sliding down the counter and into the bathroom sink, clotting around the drain in scarlet clumps.

The boy placed his palm against the mirror and *pushed*. There was a moment of sickening tension, a crackle of glass. Emrys pressed his back against the far wall, but he couldn't break the boy's gaze. The pressure behind his right eye crescendoed.

And then it was gone.

The pressure. The boy. All of it. Once again, Emrys found himself alone in the secluded bathroom, the faucet still running in the sink.

"I . . . take it you saw something?" Van Stavern asked awkwardly.

Well, nearly alone.

"What *was* that?" Emrys croaked, willing his racing heart to still.

"Hard to say without a bit more information," Van Stavern said. "In my present state, I can't sense what you do. But as I warned you in the Blue Reliquary, you and your friends are part of the hidden world now. Like it or not, that world will only become more *insistent* with time."

The Atlas cleared its nonexistent throat. "So—what did you see?"

"Brian Skupp," Emrys rasped. Though he barely knew the boy, he felt sure. And he was also sure that Brian wasn't just missing, but dead. Had that been Brian's . . . ghost? Some kind of vision? What had *happened* to him? The poor eighth grader had looked half decomposed already, but he hadn't even been missing for a week.

Whatever Emrys had just witnessed, it was enough to convince him that Brian hadn't just run away.

"There was sand," Emrys said, collecting his thoughts. "Red sand." He glanced to the open janitorial closet where he'd seen a similar pile of the stuff. But as with the mirror, the strange sediment had disappeared there, too. "Is there a . . . a relic or a monster that uses red sand? Something the Order knew about?"

"Not that I recall," Van Stavern said. "You're sure it was sand? Not ectoplasm or miasma? Or blood?"

Emrys shook his head. "I'm sure. It was red as blood, but it was definitely sand."

A phantom thought scratched at the back of Emrys's mind. Something about that felt familiar. If only he had his phone.

Outside, the warning bell shrilled. Class would be starting soon, and Emrys still had to travel two floors down. The Atlas shriveled, its eye flattening and the leather cover speckling into the familiar black-and-white pattern of a composition notebook. Emrys grabbed it and shoved it into his tote—only belatedly remembering to be gentle with Van Stavern when the book grunted in discomfort. He gave the tote an apologetic pat. But as he turned to leave the bathroom, Emrys paused, gazing into the cracked glass of the far mirror.

His right eye looked strange in the reflection—not his own. His hazel-colored iris had clouded to milky blue, like morning fog just before sunrise. The center glimmered with an eerie azure light. Emrys took a step to the side, to the nearest unbroken mirror. There, his reflection looked normal.

With a shiver, Emrys hurried to class.

✕

Emrys and Hazel had made plans to meet in the parking lot at the end of the day—once Emrys retrieved his phone. He needed to tell her about his vision as soon as possible. If Brian really *was* dead, that meant they were already dealing with a highly dangerous threat.

Was the Yellow Court involved? Van Stavern's warnings followed Emrys as he hurried past the outdoor portable classrooms. He didn't feel ready to take on the very people who'd eradicated the previous Order. If Van Stavern himself couldn't face the Whistler, what hope did three kids have?

Two, Emrys reminded himself. Serena wasn't one of them, as she'd made abundantly clear last night. Emrys just hoped the Yellow Court wouldn't do anything to make her regret her decision.

The afternoon shadows had just begun to stretch into long, umbral pillars, giving the portables an almost reverent aura. Emrys reached the door for the American History classroom and knocked, then shoved his hands into his pockets. After a long beat—vindictively long, Emrys thought—Ms. Joanna's voice finally called, "Come in!"

Emrys opened the door and was greeted by the teacher's ever-present smile.

"Can I help you, Emrys?" Ms. Joanna asked.

Emrys grimaced. They both knew why he was there, but of course she'd force him to say it.

He'd grown used to teachers not liking him, but Ms. Joanna was on another level. From his first day at Gideon, she seemed to take special pleasure in making him squirm. With her big, sweet smile and her bright, eager eyes, she reminded Emrys of a cat who'd just spotted something small and fearful to torture.

She loved Hazel, though. Maybe he just brought that out in some people, Emrys thought sadly.

"Hi," he said. "I'm here to get my phone. I mean . . . Can I have my phone back? Please?"

"Ah, yes," Ms. Joanna sighed. She opened her desk drawer and fished around inside. "I hope you aren't having any problems adjusting to our school, Emrys. A new town, a new grade level; it's a lot to take in. *And* it seems we're less relaxed about certain luxuries. Here I'm afraid, phones are a privilege, not a right."

"Thank goodness there wasn't an emergency, then," Emrys snapped, his temper rising.

All the stress of the last twenty-four hours came boiling up at once. A boy had disappeared—had *died*, Emrys knew it—and here Ms. Joanna was lecturing him about phone etiquette?

"Like, say, a missing student?" he continued sharply. "Imagine how upset my parents would have been if *I* disappeared, and they found out my *luxurious* cell phone with its tracking app had been taken from me."

Now Ms. Joanna's smile finally fell. Emrys discovered he didn't like the alternative better.

"I don't appreciate your tone, *Emrys*," the teacher practically growled.

A tense beat of silence followed, in which Emrys was sure he felt the temperature drop by a few degrees. Grown-ups didn't call kids bad names—not usually, anyway—but the way Ms. Joanna had said his name brought to mind all the insults he'd been called back in Cape Cod. It was as if the name were a disgusting taste that she couldn't scrape from her tongue quickly enough.

"Sorry . . ." he finally said in a small voice.

Ms. Joanna pulled Emrys's phone from the drawer, then set it onto the desk. She pressed a finger against the glass screen protector and slid it slowly toward him.

"Don't let me see this in my class again," she said. "It truly *would* break my heart if you didn't have it in a moment of need."

Emrys kept his eyes on the carpeted floor as he stepped forward to retrieve the phone, only glancing up when he had it in hand.

Ms. Joanna was smiling again—but something was wrong. For a brief moment, the skin of her face looked . . . off. As if it were a mask that was stretched too tight, pulling in all the wrong places. Emrys barely restrained a gasp, but he couldn't help taking an involuntary step backward.

But then the moment passed. Ms. Joanna's face was normal, her pretty smile beaming with cold delight.

"Is everything all right?" she asked.

Emrys nodded, rubbing at his right eye. Was it his imagination or had he felt it buzzing? He thought again of the Yellow Court, putting dangerous relics right where they'd be most likely to hurt people. People like Brian Skupp?

Perhaps, in his keyed-up state, Emrys was looking for threats. Or perhaps the threat was already looking back at *him*.

"Yeah," he said, turning quickly to the door. "Everything's fine."

✕

As Emrys and Hazel made their way from school, he breathlessly recounted the strange experience in the bathroom, careful to keep his voice down whenever they passed teachers or clumps of other students heading home.

Hazel listened somberly, frowning at every gruesome detail.

"I'd say you were hallucinating," she remarked as he finished, "if not for what we experienced last night."

"Something happened to Brian," Emrys insisted. "Something horrible. I just know it."

He lifted his phone and was greeted by nearly a dozen text messages from Serena. The last one read: *HELLO?? ARE YOU TWO STILL ALIVE? Emrys don't ignore this! I know you're off in HOO-HA HORROR LAND!!! Tell Hazel I NEED TO TALK.*

He swiped the notification away with a spike of guilt. He'd get back to her soon, but right now, he needed answers. Serena was a popular kid at a fancy private school. She probably had a small army of friends and guidance counselors ready to talk her through any anxious spells. She could deal for a little while longer.

And Emrys had a mystery to solve.

He opened the New Rotterdam Wiki search page.

"Does red sand sound familiar?" he asked Hazel. "I swear I remember it from somewhere."

Hazel thought about it for a moment, then her eyes brightened.

"Search for 'Wandering Hour,'" she suggested.

Emrys keyed in the name and the article came right up. He held his phone up for Hazel and they scanned the page together. Both gasped at the same time.

"This has *got* to be it!" Emrys said.

"Oh wow . . ." Hazel rasped.

"What?" Van Stavern's voice blurted from the tote. "What did you find?"

"*Shhh!*" Emrys hissed, pulling it close. "We're still in public. We'll tell you soon."

He glanced at Hazel. "We need to regroup. Do some research and plan our next move."

She nodded, pulling out her own phone. "I'll text Serena."

Emrys awkwardly cleared his throat. "Are you sure?" he asked. "Last night she seemed pretty upset. And her texts today . . . There were a lot of all-caps messages."

Hazel shrugged, her eyes on her screen. "She'll come around. Trust me, I've known her since we were toddlers. And it's not like we can just drop her as a friend because she doesn't want to join the Order. She can help with research."

Emrys nodded reluctantly, though Hazel didn't see it.

Not for the first time, he felt an uncomfortable itch of jealousy creeping in. When he'd first moved to New Rotterdam, it hadn't really occurred to Emrys that Hazel would already have friends here, even best friends. It should have. And while he'd tried with Serena, he really had, last night only widened the gap that already existed between them. Instead of three friends on a mission, they were now two inverse sets—natural and supernatural—with Hazel linking them at the center. How long could such a strange Venn diagram really survive?

Emrys shook his head. He was being ridiculous. This was bigger than their middle-school drama. Much bigger.

He glanced toward the school entrance . . .

And gasped.

The two police officers from the morning were still there, but now they were looking right at Emrys and Hazel. There was the tall, reedy one—Emrys noticed his thin teeth were set far apart, almost like a child's drawing of a mouth. The other, a man with brown skin and wide-set eyes, was as dense and silent as ooze. Neither moved—they simply watched.

A fly trap and a pitcher plant, Emrys thought. The two just seemed . . . carnivorous.

"Hazel," Emrys whispered urgently. "Hazel . . . *look*."

Hazel glanced up toward the police, then took a step back. "Why are they looking at us like that?" she whispered.

The invisible world doesn't like being seen.

Like it or not, that world will only become more insistent with time.

Van Stavern's warnings echoed in Emrys's mind. The buzzing behind his right eye had returned, this time he was sure.

"Do you feel that?" he asked.

". . . Yes," Hazel said, absently touching a finger to her temple.

Was this the "double-edged sword" Van Stavern had mentioned? Could even the New Rotterdam police, the adults sworn to protect everyone, be part of the danger? Perhaps the Order's mysterious second sight was already revealing things Emrys would rather not have known.

"Let's just get out of here," he said.

Hazel nodded. The two of them walked past the school entrance, trying to appear casual as they left the grounds.

But Emrys felt the officers' eyes on him the whole way out.

The Wandering Hour

From the New Rotterdam Wiki Project

The Wandering Hour is the name given to a phenomenon that is little understood and all but impossible to document. Its survivors are few in number, whereas its victims are uncountable and unverifiable.

At the heart of the mystery is a strange object: an hourglass containing red sand. Witnesses have described the sand's hue as being anywhere from a bright scarlet to a dark, purplish maroon. But all accounts agree that setting eyes on the hourglass is tantamount to a death sentence.

Its first documented appearance comes from a 1965 estate sale, where it was listed among the personal effects of sixty-two-year-old Edna Milton. Edna had opened her home to more than a dozen foster children between 1962 and 1964, and at least five of those children went missing under her care. Edna herself disappeared and was presumed dead in 1964. The strange red-sand hourglass found among her belongings vanished shortly before it could be put up for sale.

Although the missing children were assumed to have run away, it is possible that they may have been the earliest victims of the Wandering Hour, along with Edna Milton herself.

The hourglass resurfaced under tragic circumstances in 1968. Teenage sweethearts Biff Bentley and Betty Grimm were eating ice cream in Arcadia Park when Betty noticed the hourglass nearby. She called it to Biff's attention, and as he took a closer look, something uncanny happened. The red sand, which had been gathered entirely in the top bulb of the hourglass, suddenly appeared in the bottom bulb instead. It was as if the hourglass had run its course in the time it took Biff to blink. Even more alarming, Betty was gone, with only a melted ice cream to indicate she'd ever been there. Betty was never seen again, and although there was no evidence to indict him, Biff lived under the suspicion that he had murdered the love of his life until he died of a heart attack at the age of forty-three.

No further mention of the hourglass appears in any records until December of 1984, when teenager Enoch Pierce was found floating in the waters of Cimmerian Bay. Suffering from hypothermia and shock, Enoch was taken to Saint Azazel Hospital, where he reportedly shared an incoherent story of being pursued across town by a ravenous monster. Further details of the tale he told were not recorded, but for a brief time following the incident, Enoch became a frequent presence at various NRPD precincts, where he insisted that the children of New Rotterdam were being eaten alive and that police should seek out and destroy a red-sand hourglass. Records indicate he spent at least one night in jail for disturbing the peace.

Many years later, in 2003, thirteen-year-old Emma Winthrop disappeared from her mother's side during a grocery trip—only to reappear minutes later, wild-eyed and battered, all the way across town on the outskirts of Effigy Grove. Emma told a confused tale about an hourglass set amongst sugary cereal, a witch with snake fangs, and a desperate flight for her life that lasted "about an hour," despite the fact she'd been missing for only minutes. Emma's story was soundly dismissed by her furious parents, but Emma remained vocal about her experience online, until she was institutionalized for psychosis and paranoid delusions at the age of eighteen. It was Emma who first coined the term "the Wandering Hour" in a poem that she shared online before her accounts were deactivated in 2008: "Make not a sound beneath the bower / Still your heart as you there cower / Else fork-tongued witch will hear the clangor / You'll not survive the Wand'ring Hour."

The red-sand hourglass has not been seen since, but the New Rotterdam Department of Child Welfare estimates that roughly two dozen youth go missing in New Rotterdam each year. Official statistics list the vast majority of those youth as runaways, although there is some debate about the accuracy of those statistics, and city officials have come under fire for being too quick to declare missing-persons cases closed. How many of these so-called runaways might have fallen victim to the "fork-tongued witch" inside the Wandering Hour, we may never know.

9

"You're serious?" said Van Stavern. "All that information . . . the Wandering Hour, details from the incident report, the victims' names . . . it's all right there on your *phone*?"

"Not on his phone, exactly," said Hazel. "It's on the internet. We're able to use our phones to access—"

"I know what the *internet* is," snapped Van Stavern. "Honestly, it's like you children think I hail from some distant century."

"Sorry!" Hazel said, and then, leaning in toward Emrys, she whispered, "I just thought he was more of a *book* guy."

Emrys grinned despite himself. Hazel knew he was always up for a corny joke, even if their lives might be in peril.

"Those in the Order are meant to be the keepers of knowledge concerning those relics," said Van Stavern. "It is disconcerting to think that this *wiki* might be a more reliable source of information. Who is responsible for it?"

"Nobody," Emrys answered. "And everybody. The whole point of a wiki is that it's updated and maintained by the people who use it. Hazel and I have contributed, actually. A little bit."

"How very democratic. It must be *rife* with misinformation." Van Stavern's gaze focused on Emrys. "Just as long as you don't divulge any secrets."

Emrys blushed. "Of course not. But speaking of secrets . . . are you sure we should be talking in broad daylight?"

Even as he said it, Emrys realized "broad daylight" was overstating things a bit. The scant sunlight that shone through the overhead gauze of clouds was cold and diffuse. But his point remained: he and Hazel were out in public, sitting upon a bench, the Atlas set between them in its undisguised state.

"It's New Rotterdam," Hazel said, by way of answering. "People mind their own business to a fault."

Emrys took in the scene before him. They were in the Shallows, a bustling shopping district situated between their school and home. But while they were surrounded by people coming and going, those people all kept their heads down and their eyes averted. Some wore masks covering their mouths and noses; others wore little earbuds, and they moved to their own personal soundtracks. Back in Cape Cod, people had greeted their neighbors and smiled at strangers. Not so in New Rotterdam. No one spared a glance for the kids on the bench, or their unsettlingly bound book.

No one except the startlingly intense girl cutting a swath through the foot traffic, stomping right toward them.

"Serena—" began Emrys.

"Oh good, you remember my name," Serena said, and though Emrys hurriedly picked up the Atlas to make room for her on the bench, she remained standing, looming over them. "The way you ignored my texts, I thought maybe the brainwashing had set in completely."

"You know I keep my phone off during the day," Hazel said.

"And I also know you never met a rule you did not embrace with your whole heart." She turned her gaze on Emrys. "That's why I texted our mutual *friend*."

"My teacher took my phone," Emrys said meekly. He didn't like the weird emphasis she'd put on the word "friend." Like she didn't really mean it.

"A boy at our school went missing," Hazel said, drawing Serena's attention back onto her. "We think . . . we have reason to believe he's . . ."

"He's dead," said Emrys, and though he spoke quietly, the words were too loud in his ears—too final. He hadn't known Brian, and this terrible knowledge felt far too intimate to have fallen to him to share. "Who's going to tell his parents?"

"This boy," said Serena. "He's dead because of these . . . relics?"

"One relic in particular," answered Van Stavern.

"Ah-ah!" said Serena. "I'm talking to my friends, not the encyclops-pedia."

Well, okay, thought Emrys. At least he rated above Van Stavern.

Hazel passed her phone to Serena—she must have pulled up the wiki entry, too. While Serena read, Hazel squeezed Emrys's hand. "We need a plan," she said, adjusting her headband. "We can't just crisscross town until our spooky-sense starts tingling."

"The survivors could tell us more," Emrys suggested.

Hazel bit her lip. "Like Emma Winthrop? My mom might be able to access the psychiatric hospital's records." She sighed. "But it feels wrong. Like we'd be retraumatizing her."

"Only one of the victims was committed, though," Emrys reminded her. "There was another guy, Enoch something."

"Pierce," said Serena, returning Hazel's phone. She looked pointedly at Hazel, but Hazel only shrugged. "Mr. Pierce?" Serena prompted. "He owns the antique store down the block."

Emrys bounded off the bench. "Wait, really? Are you sure?"

Serena rolled her shoulders. "Sure, I'm sure. My dads have bought enough furniture from him over the years. He's weird, but I always thought it was, like, *normal* weird. Not survived-an-encounter-with-a-murderous-timepiece weird."

"You know him?" Emrys gripped Serena's elbow. "Serena, you *have* to come with us."

"On the contrary." Serena pulled free of his grip. "It's you *two* who will come with me. With any luck, Mr. Pierce will convince you to forget you ever heard of these relics." She grinned. "And if we're *really* lucky, he'll be in the market for old, creepy books."

Enoch Pierce, to Emrys's eye, wasn't weird at all. A tall, white man with graying temples and a neat sweater vest, he greeted them with a smile—one that deepened when he recognized Serena. He asked after her parents, and while they talked, Emrys allowed his eyes to drift over the shop.

There was furniture everywhere, wardrobes pressed back-to-back and crammed between bed frames and desks. Chairs were set atop tables, sharing the surfaces with lamps, pots, globes, delicate teacups . . . even a taxidermied beaver. Space was at a premium in New Rotterdam, where the average building was over a hundred years old, and shops made do with what they had.

It reminded Emrys of the Order's reliquary, only wilder and more cramped. He realized with some dismay how easily a relic could be hidden there . . . but no. There was no telltale buzz behind his eye. Either his new senses were still developing or everything in the shop was utterly mundane.

Hazel turned the beaver around. "What?" she said, at Emrys's questioning look. "I didn't like how it was looking at me."

"I'll tell my dads about the escritoire, I promise," Serena was saying. "But my friends and I . . . we're here for another reason."

"Oh?" said Mr. Pierce. He smiled again, but on seeing their stony looks, his smile faltered. "What is it?"

Emrys hesitated. Somehow, knowing that the unseen world was real didn't make it any easier to talk about it. And if the wiki was right, Mr. Pierce had plenty of reason not to want to hear anything about it.

Hazel picked up the slack. "We're doing research," she said. "Trying to find a . . . an hourglass. An hourglass with red sand."

Mr. Pierce's expression hardened. "We were online, and we saw your name, and—"

"I don't talk about that," said Mr. Pierce. "Who are you, again?"

"They're with me," Serena said quickly. "Sorry. We know how rumors can get out of hand. Especially online. What we read, it probably isn't even true—"

"It's true." Mr. Pierce's eyes locked on Serena. "I know what story you mean. It's all true. But it was a long time ago. A different life . . ."

"Please," said Hazel. "It's important. Anything you can tell us, anything at all."

Emrys stepped forward. "A boy at our school is d—"

"He's *missing*," Serena interrupted.

Emrys nodded. "Right. Missing. And I . . . I saw something. Red sand . . ."

Serena shot him a look. That was new information to her.

Mr. Pierce sighed wearily. "I always hope that it's over. That she's gone. But she's never gone for long."

"She?" prompted Emrys.

At the sound of his voice, Mr. Pierce snapped to attention. He turned on his heel and strode quickly to the door. Emrys worried he was about to throw them out. Instead, the man locked the dead bolt, and, peering through the glass door, he turned a sign over from OPEN to CLOSED.

"Wait a minute—" said Serena. She stepped forward, but Hazel put a steadying hand on her elbow.

"Hold on, Serena," she whispered. "It's okay."

"You have to understand." Mr. Pierce turned away from the door to look at the three of them, one after another. "The last time I told anybody this story, I was thrown into jail. People don't want to hear this."

"We do," said Hazel.

Emrys nodded, gripping the straps of his tote.

"Yeah," Serena said, but she sounded hesitant. "Go on."

"It was December, 1984. Just before Christmas. I had been playing football at the YMCA." He shook his head. "My dad's idea. I never liked football. I was alone in the locker room, the last one to leave. And I looked up, and . . . there was this hourglass, just sitting there on the bench. Seemed to have come from nowhere. I still wonder who left it there."

Emrys's throat went dry. It was monstrous to imagine someone leaving a dangerous relic where it was bound to hurt someone. But according to Van Stavern, the Yellow Court routinely did that exact thing.

"What did you do?" asked Hazel.

"Nothing," he answered. "I noticed it was broken—clogged up, I figured. I almost flicked the glass, but then thought better of it. I figured it had to belong to somebody, and that the owner would be back to pick it up. I didn't want to be accused of anything. But then the sand started moving."

"You didn't touch it?" Hazel asked. "You're sure?"

"I'm sure," Mr. Pierce answered. "I was still a few feet away."

Hazel shot Emrys a look, and he knew what she was thinking. If the relic triggered its trap without physical contact, then anyone who even looked at the thing was in danger. How were they supposed to retrieve it without looking at it?

"As soon as the sand started to fall, I just . . . I knew something was wrong. Even before the old lady showed up."

"Old lady?" said Emrys. "In the locker room?"

"I figured she was lost. Harmless." He winced. "Till she spoke. And her voice, something in it, it just set off every alarm bell in my brain. Without even thinking about it, I picked up my football helmet and threw it right at her. And that's when things got weird."

Serena made a small noise as she swallowed back a sarcastic comment.

"The helmet—it never made it. I mean, it just stopped, midthrow, and it *hovered* there in the air." Mr. Pierce's eyes had a faraway look, as if he were seeing the scene unfold before him all over again.

"The helmet," said Emrys. "You said you picked it up? You hadn't been holding it the whole time?"

"Does that matter?" Serena asked pointedly.

"I don't know, Serena," Emrys said, a little hotly. "Maybe."

Mr. Pierce shook his head. "I can't say for sure. It was a long time ago."

"That's all right, Mr. Pierce," said Hazel. "What happened next?"

"I panicked and ran out onto the street, right into traffic. I probably would have been hit by a car, except none of the cars were moving. None of the people were moving. Everybody, every single person, was frozen in place, just like that football helmet."

Serena scoffed. "How is that possible?"

Mr. Pierce lost his faraway look. His gaze refocused on her. "I told you. You don't want to hear this. Not really."

"Maybe not," Emrys said. "But we *need* to hear it." He turned to Serena. "Right?"

Serena crossed her arms. "Right," she said. "Sorry, Mr. Pierce."

"The old woman," said Hazel. "*She* could move."

"That's right," said Mr. Pierce. "And she seemed to be everywhere at once. Behind me one second, then ahead of me the next. She was laughing the whole time." He withdrew a handkerchief and dabbed at the sweat beading on his forehead. "I was fast back then—in good shape. She was faster."

Emrys frowned at the idea of an elderly woman outpacing a young athlete. Seemingly *toying* with him.

"I couldn't outrun her, so I hid. The idea came to me at the wharf. I thought, I don't know, I thought maybe she was following my scent. I know how that sounds, but there was something . . . something inhuman . . ." He shuddered, closing his eyes and taking a moment before continuing. "So I waded into the water—it was freezing cold, I mean *freezing*—and I hid beneath the old pier, treading water for an hour. Long enough that I didn't even feel the cold, after a while. I couldn't feel anything except blind terror. That never dulled. I still feel it, sometimes, as I'm just about to drift off to sleep."

"But she didn't find you," Emrys said, eager for the happy ending. "You got away."

"It was a near thing. She never stopped looking. I could hear her, calling my name. She said she was going to eat me, and I believed her." He licked his lips. "But it was worse when she was quiet. I kept expecting to see her sagging face, peering down at me through a crack in the pier. Or to feel her bony fingers beneath the water, gripping my ankles. I—" His voice cracked. He cleared his throat. "It was so quiet that I could hear her searching for me. It didn't sound like footsteps though. It sounded . . . it sounded like slithering . . ."

"She knew your name," said Hazel.

"Yeah," said Mr. Pierce. "She said it in the locker room, too. She was trying to trick me into trusting her."

"What happened next?" Hazel asked.

"I passed out. I guess some fishermen pulled me from the water, once the hour was up. Next thing I knew, I woke up in the hospital. Took a long time to believe that I was safe."

"What did you tell people?" asked Emrys.

"I told them the truth. At first. But it was easier to believe it had all been a hallucination, brought on by hypothermia. Easier for everyone but me." He grimaced. "The worst part was when other kids started disappearing—all from the neighborhood around my YMCA. Not one of them was more than half a mile away. I knew what happened to those kids. She got them. She killed them, most likely. But nobody ever found any trace of them. And the more I insisted that it was the hourglass . . . that an old woman was using it to stop time for an hour to hunt down kids . . . the more I saw folks grow cold. Suspicious. I wore out their sympathy real quick." He sighed. "They stopped calling it hallucinations. Started accusing me of doing it all for attention, trying to . . . I don't know . . . *attach* myself to other people's tragedy.

"When the cops started treating me like a criminal, I finally got the message and shut my mouth. It got easier after the disappearances ended. No internet back then, but there was a missing-persons board up at the YMCA. A month went by without a new poster, and then another, and I figured the old woman was gone. Moved on, maybe. Or . . ." He grimaced again. "Or she had her fill."

Emrys saw Hazel start to say something, but she hesitated. "What is it?" he prompted. "What are you thinking?"

"I'm thinking . . . maybe Edna Milton wasn't a victim of this thing. Maybe she's behind it all."

"The old woman from the article?" Serena shook her head. "She'd be over a hundred."

"Unless she can literally freeze time," Hazel said. "Or, I don't know . . . maybe she's a ghost haunting the hourglass. Maybe she isn't human anymore."

"All good theories," said Emrys. Then, remembering they were in the presence of a traumatized survivor, he said, "I mean, your theories have merit. None of this is *good*."

"Why would she come back now?" Serena cast a suspicious look at Emrys's tote bag, as if directing the question at Van Stavern. "After all this time?"

"Maybe she got hungry," said Mr. Pierce flatly.

Emrys felt queasy. If Edna Milton was feeding . . .

How many kids would it take to sate her?

"Thank you, Mr. Pierce," said Hazel. "For telling us your story. This is more than we'd hoped for."

"We should go," Emrys said. "It'll be dark soon."

"Of course," said Mr. Pierce. He unlocked the dead bolt and opened the door. "Just . . . be careful out there, all right?" He smiled wanly. "And tell your dads about that escritoire, Serena. It really is a stellar piece."

"I will," she promised. "But . . . just one more thing. You said this whole . . . *ordeal* lasted for an hour. That's awfully precise . . ."

"An hour. Precisely." Mr. Pierce pulled back his sleeve to reveal an old analogue watch. "My dad's watch. I still wear it, for luck. And I was wearing it that day. When I woke up in the hospital, this watch was exactly one hour ahead."

"The Wandering Hour," Emrys said, breathless.

"Funny," said Mr. Pierce quietly. "It felt longer." He closed the door behind them.

The Orchid from Outer Space

From the New Rotterdam Wiki Project

McNee's Flower Emporium holds the record for the longest-running shop in New Rotterdam, open from 1931 until its closure in May 1964. Barnabas McNee, the sole proprietor, grew up in the neighborhood informally known as the Shallows, then a loose collection of public houses for seasonal fishermen.

During its first decade of existence, the shop earned meager returns. The Shallows was not yet the affluent shopping district it would become, and what plants Barnabas could source at the time were local blooms, most of them grown in his home garden behind the business. That all changed the night of the 1940 Meteor Shower.

While watching the falling stars from the shore with his sweetheart, a young woman named Aubrey Halfurd, Barnabas came across what he later claimed was a mysterious seed. Upon planting the seed in his garden, Barnabas was surprised at how it took to the arid New Rotterdam soil, quickly sprouting into a full, blooming orchid plant.

But what set this particular plant apart were the small, thornlike growths that lined the center of every bloom—each pointed and red, like rows of blood-stained teeth. Barnabas named his new discovery *Cymbidium aubreyi*, after his sweetheart. (The plant was never officially designated as a new species, however. Barnabas refused to surrender it to scientists from the Smithsonian Museum.)

McNee quickly capitalized on the bloom, dubbing it "the Orchid from Outer Space" and advertising its existence in the local papers. Curious onlookers flooded the shop. Soon Barnabas was earning enough to source rare blossoms from around the world and transform McNee's Flower Emporium from a local flower shop into a purveyor of exotic plants and hybrids.

It was at the height of Barnabas's success, however, that Aubrey Halfurd vanished. What happened to Barnabas's love remains a mystery, though her disappearance had a profound effect on the man. He became reclusive, rarely venturing from the leaf-choked twilight of the shop. Most believed Aubrey simply left Barnabas, no longer inclined to wilt in the business's shadow.

But Aubrey was only the first disappearance connected to Barnabas. In the twenty years that followed, nine individuals went missing. One, a shop clerk named Symon Krelbin, even approached police with suspicions about his boss, claiming to have spied him feeding hunks of meat to the now-famous orchid. Symon disappeared the following week. Though police questioned Barnabas, no evidence was ever found to implicate him.

Barnabas abruptly closed the shop in 1964, locking himself inside the doors. Concerned for the man's health, a neighbor visited one morning and found the front door open and the shop abandoned. Most of the plants had withered from neglect, except for the orchid. It alone stood tall and healthy, practically overgrown.

The neighbor reported an uneasy feeling at the sight of all those blossoms grinning with bloody jaws. She claimed the plant looked "hungry." She hurried home and alerted the authorities to McNee's disappearance. When emergency services arrived, however, they found no sign of the shopkeeper *or* his prized bloom.

10

Despite Mr. Pierce's harrowing account of the Wandering Hour—and the nauseating horror of what that meant for Edna Milton's victims—Emrys found he was now buzzing with excitement.

He marched ahead of Hazel and Serena, then pivoted around to face the girls.

"This is it," he said. All around them, the shops in the Shallows were closing for the evening, windows and doorways blinking out like snuffed candles. "Not only do we have proof that the red-sand hourglass exists, we've found a lead for tracking it."

"A lead?" asked Serena. "How do you figure? All I heard was a sad story about an old lady who *eats kids*."

Emrys shook his head. "Mr. Pierce said the disappearances in his time were all in a specific area—the neighborhood around the YMCA. But Gideon, where Brian was last seen, is nowhere near there."

Serena quirked a brow. "So?"

"So maybe Edna—or the Hour or whatever—moves around, hunting in a particular territory before going dormant."

Hazel's eyes lit up. "If we can figure out her territory, then we'll know where to look. We might even be able to sense her with our Order powers."

Emrys nodded. "Exactly! Let's head home. We can check if anyone else has gone missing recently. Maybe someone from the wiki would know. Oh! I bet Mom and Dad would let you both stay over for dinner, too."

Hazel frowned. "Sorry, Em, but I'm hanging with my mom tonight. She's got the night off from the hospital, so we're going out to dinner." Hazel lifted her phone, frowning at the time. "Actually, I should go. We're supposed to meet at Pepe's Pies in half an hour."

Emrys fought to keep his expression neutral, but in that moment he empathized with Mr. Pierce's story about plunging into the freezing cold ocean, at least a little. He glanced nervously at Serena. Hazel was leaving them? Alone?

"Right!" he said. "Of course! Have a good dinner. We'll, uh, text."

"Whatever *that's* worth," Serena muttered.

With a nod, Hazel shifted her backpack onto her shoulders and turned north, in the opposite direction of their building. In moments, she was gone.

Emrys, meanwhile, turned to Serena. "So!" he said, attempting to keep the mood light. "You want to google for disappearances while I check the wiki chat?"

Based on the withering look he received, Emrys suspected she did not favor this plan.

The wind had gone quiet. Emrys found the stillness far louder than the usual howling seaside gales. In just a few months, he'd gotten used to New Rotterdam—to its cold fog and crashing waves. Even to its monsters. And now Alyx Van Stavern had given him something far better than familiarity—a true key to the city.

Power. Agency. The ability to change things for the better.

Finally, it felt like Emrys *belonged* in New Rotterdam. So why couldn't he and Serena find the same sense of belonging? She had so *many* friends. All Emrys had was this.

She brushed past him, walking until her back was to Emrys. Then she stopped.

"I saw things, too, you know," she said.

Emrys frowned. "What do you mean?"

"Today, at school. Horrible things. I saw *hands* try to push through a whiteboard in third period. During gym, this woman entered the room wearing an old-timey nightgown. Bizarre, but it wasn't until my eye started twitching that I realized something was *really* wrong." Serena took a deep breath. "Her whole body was burned. And the moment she noticed *me* noticing *her*, she opened her mouth to scream—but no noise came out. Just a thick plume of smoke. That's when *I* started screaming."

Serena whirled around, her eyes wide with real fear. "My friends looked at me like I was having a fit. And who could blame them? I was! I tried texting all day, but neither of you would answer. And I couldn't talk to anyone else about it, could I? Who would have believed me? So I was alone with these . . . *visions*, just trying not to panic every time I turned a corner!"

"I'm sorry . . ." Emrys said flimsily. "A teacher really did take my phone."

"This is just going to keep happening, isn't it?" Serena asked. "We'll see monsters and shadows and—and *freaks* everywhere we go."

Emrys flinched from the harsh word, but what could he do but nod? "Probably."

"Then why do you seem so happy about it, Emrys?"

Serena's gaze changed now, cold fear igniting into something else. Something hotter.

"Is this *fun* for you?" she asked pointedly. "That awful book has tossed us alone into the ocean, and you can't seem to *wait* to drown."

"That's not . . ." Emrys faltered, taking a step back.

"Isn't it? You heard Mr. Pierce's story. That thing *eats* people. They disappear and no one ever sees them again. They're just forgotten! But rather than running *away* from something that awful and unbeatable, you want to run *toward* it—and take Hazel with you!" Serena shook her head. "Mark my words, Emrys. By the time this is over, one of you will be dead."

Emrys crossed his arms, narrowing his eyes. He remembered what Van Stavern had told them the night before. "This is happening, Serena," he said, "whether we want it to or not."

"That's exactly the problem!" Serena threw her hands into the air. "You *do* want it! For some twisted reason, you want it so much! Probably because you're a creepy little *weirdo*."

Emrys recoiled like he'd been slapped. Even Serena seemed to recognize she'd gone too far. The anger fled from her eyes, replaced with what looked almost like surprise. Then her expression hardened.

Again, she turned her back on Emrys. "I'll take the long way home," she said flatly. "Google how to get eaten on your own."

And with that, she was gone, marching away from the Shallows. The wind picked up, a held breath finally released. Emrys stood alone on an empty street, in a town where he didn't belong at all.

Emrys's mom greeted him from the living room when he arrived.

"Hey, hon! How was school?"

So the school hadn't informed parents about Brian's disappearance yet. His mom would have mentioned it, otherwise. Emrys wondered if they *ever* planned to. Maybe that was just how things worked here. His mind flashed to the mugs and T-shirts filling the New Rotterdam gift shops, cheerfully depicting real-life monsters. It was a lot less fun now, knowing each jokey souvenir might represent countless lost lives. Lives the people of New Rotterdam seemed all too happy to sweep aside.

Lives like Brian Skupp's.

"Good," Emrys lied, with a small pang of guilt.

"I'm on a work deadline, so your dad's cooking tonight," Emrys's mom said. "But want to watch a movie after dinner? Nothing scary, sorry."

"Actually, I have some work to do, too," Emrys said. "School project. Maybe tomorrow?"

"It's a date."

Back in his room, Emrys scrolled through the tenth page of search results for missing persons, frowning into the glowing screen. The usual search engines hadn't turned up much. Apparently local disappearances didn't always make the news, either. Mostly he was getting a bunch of ads for unrelated vacation rentals.

At least he'd been able to find a photo of Edna Milton. Despite her ghoulish entry in the wiki, the woman pictured looked . . . nice. Unassuming. Emrys supposed this was partially why no one had suspected her for so long.

Hopefully the wiki contributors would know more about recent disappearances. He opened the StrifeChat window where he'd posted his question about missing locals, but no one had responded yet.

The New Rotterdam Wiki Project had a dedicated chat server for those with mod privileges, where they could compare notes, discuss articles, and—more frequently—talk about nothing in particular. Emrys wasn't *technically* old enough to use StrifeChat, but he rarely logged in anyway. Only when he had a real question for the wiki community, like now. His parents wouldn't be happy with him if they saw the chat window, though. There were plenty of people who used the anonymity of the internet to hurt others, but Emrys knew better than to trust strangers online. He knew it better than some grown-ups, he figured.

As soon as he got his answer, he'd exit the chat.

"Emrys . . ." Van Stavern sighed from his perch on the bookshelf, surrounded by Emrys's collection of square-headed Jazzo-Bop! horror figurines. Emrys had found it necessary to keep the Atlas high out of Sir Galahound's reach. The dog had developed an instant curiosity for the talking, blinking book. Even now, his tail wagged at the sound of Van Stavern's voice.

"That was quite a conversation you had with Serena earlier. Are you all right? Do you want to . . . ? What I mean to say is . . . Oh, I was never good at these things."

"It's fine," Emrys said, keeping his eyes squarely on the computer screen. "Not the first time someone's called me that. And let's face it, it won't be the last."

Van Stavern lapsed into silence, but Emrys found the quiet was worse. It just provided better acoustics for Serena's insult to keep ringing in his ears. After a moment, he spun his chair around to face the book.

"You know, Serena was right about one thing," Emrys said. "I shouldn't go jumping into danger without some way to protect myself and Hazel. Is there anything in there that I could use to fight Edna? Like, Magic Missile or something?"

The book blinked slowly at him. "I'm going to pretend that you did not just quote a first-level Dungeons & Dragons spell at me and simply show you the standard hex I used when situations became volatile."

As in the bathroom at school, the Atlas flipped open of its own accord, pages fluttering by in rapid succession. Emrys stood from his desk chair and made his way to the book. Words were inscribed at the top of the page in looping cursive. The text that followed was as dense as a brick wall.

"Pror-ror luh tiss-a-gee?" Emrys sounded out.

"This . . . may take a while," Van Stavern's voice sounded from the book. "*Pourrir le tissage*—'rot the weave.' A hex that tugs at the very strings of reality. Anything caught within its energies will be pulled apart at the quantum level."

"What does that mean?" Emrys asked.

"It blasts things to bits. I developed the spell myself and added it to the Atlas with my own hand. As the *new* bearer of the Atlas, you are empowered by its magic. You alone can learn the spells within. In theory, anyway."

"What's all this writing below it?"

"Instructions for entering the meditative state necessary to perceive the threads that make up our fragile reality, followed by the hex's incantations, both short- and long-form. Once you've mastered the longer incantations, you can utilize the shorter command words for quick application in the field."

"So I meditate and then I say some words. Got it." Emrys flipped the page. "Wait—these incantations are in French!"

"*Oui,*" Van Stavern answered dryly.

Emrys spent the next half hour attempting to enter the trance state described in the Atlas, but couldn't perceive much beyond Sir Galahound's eager, curious muzzle nosing into his line of sight. Next, he tried the incantations, but found the French even more difficult to grasp than the Latin from earlier that day. Every new consonant melted against his tongue, like a bite from a snow cone that disappeared as soon as he had it.

"This is impossible!" Emrys grumbled. He threw himself back onto his bed.

"If the impossible is what you mean to command," Van Stavern said, "then it is what you must achieve." Then, after a beat, he added, "You're distracted."

Emrys exhaled toward the ceiling, but he couldn't disagree.

Finally, he sat up. "They called me weird in my old town, too," he said, picking at his comforter. "Whether it was my anxiety or my ADHD, I always seemed to be too much or not enough. Too focused on the wrong things. It wasn't until Hazel and I met at camp that I found someone who really *got* me. I thought . . . I thought maybe New Rotterdam would be better. I became a little obsessed with it, I guess. In a place where weird is ordinary, maybe I'd finally fit in. But it hasn't been like that at all. Even with monsters and magic, I'm still me, and other people are still other people."

The pages of the Atlas flipped closed, the book's eerie blue eye narrowing upon Emrys.

"You have an unquiet mind," Van Stavern intoned. "I understand that better than you know. You're far from the first aspiring sorcerer to think differently, Emrys. It's practically a prerequisite."

"I'm tired of feeling weird," Emrys said.

"That word again." The book chuckled. Emrys realized it was the first time he'd heard Van Stavern laugh. It was a bit unsettling, truth be told. "Do you know its origin? Originally it meant *fate*. Destiny. Weird is our charter, Emrys. As witches and wizards, we sculpt fate to our liking. The weird is ours to *wield*. It is only through embracing it that you will come into your full—"

"I thought you said there was math."

"—oh, enough about the math! Honestly, you're more afraid of a little algebra than the child-eating monster. But what I'm saying is, for all my talk of ancient languages and wicked equations, the truth is that sorcery isn't science. It wants to tell a story—a *strange* story—and true mastery is just about letting it tell that story through you. *Pourrir le tissage* was my spell. It worked for me. You will need to find your own way into this tale."

Before Emrys had a chance to process this odd bit of advice, a ping sounded from his computer. He leapt up from his bed, opening the StrifeChat window.

Someone had replied to his question! A user named @TheGatekeeper. Emrys recognized the handle from the wiki. They'd edited tons of articles.

> Looking into disappearances, huh? Be careful, @EmDash! We all know that digging for answers in NR can quickly lead to digging your own grave. Mwa ha ha ha. Kidding aside, there were several odd ones in the last few weeks. Young folks, mostly. Awful stuff. You won't find these in the news, of course, but below

are some links to the social pages of their friends and
family. Probably a better place to start researching.

As soon as Emrys finished reading, a private message notification popped up. Someone had DMed him? He clicked into
his inbox, where a user named @AmberBishop had sent a note.
Emrys didn't recognize *this* handle. The profile picture was of
a gold-colored chess piece.

> @EmDash Are you researching for a particular
> article in the wiki? Which one? Maybe I can help.

Emrys nearly found himself replying that he was looking
into the Wandering Hour, but then thought better of it. As much
as he loved the wiki community, his loyalty was to the Order
now. Van Stavern had warned him about revealing sensitive
secrets. Maybe once they put a stop to Edna, it would be safe
to share more.

Emrys typed out a quick reply.

> @AmberBishop Just some general research. Might
> have more soon. THANKS!!

Then he opened the social media links and quickly logged
out. Scanning through, Emrys was surprised by the number.

Including Brian, six people had gone missing in eight weeks, and yet nothing had made the news. Most of the families seemed *sure* their loved ones hadn't just up and left, and nearly all described the police response to the "runaways" as being half-hearted at best. (Usually with much ruder language.) Emrys finally had to close the posts entirely. They made him too sad.

So Serena was right about something else, too. New Rotterdam seemed eager to forget these poor people, the oldest of which was just a college student.

So far, Brian was the youngest.

Emrys opened the map app on his phone and dropped pins where each of the missing had last been seen. When he got to the final address, he paused.

Casper Leonard, the college student, had been just a block away when he'd disappeared *last night*. He'd taken a bag of dirty clothes to the nearby laundromat and was quietly studying during the spin cycle. He never emptied the laundry and never made it home.

Emrys drew a line with his finger across the various pinned sites. As he suspected, they were all clumped pretty closely together. Was this the territory Edna was hunting in?

Emrys frowned. His own apartment building was so close. Was it too close? He couldn't be sure yet. There weren't enough data points. He needed to talk with Hazel first thing, though. If all these disappearances really were connected to the Wandering Hour, then Edna's hunting ground might be just under their noses. Maybe they could find her before she claimed anyone else.

Or, Emrys thought with a chill, *maybe she'll find us.*

Mark my words, Emrys. Serena's warning tolled through his thoughts like a bell. *By the time this is over, one of you will be dead.*

It had the uncomfortable weight of a prophecy. Looking down at the map clustered with blood-red pins marking young lives that had been cut short, Emrys was keenly aware of how powerless he still was against the forces that hunted in this town. There was so much he didn't know—including how to fight against them. He needed to learn fast.

A knock on his bedroom door jarred him from his worries. Emrys cast a quick glance to the Atlas, but it already looked like a simple notebook.

"Come in!" he called.

Emrys's dad poked his head in. "Whoa, pretty dark in here, guy. Turn on a light so you don't wear your eyes out, okay?"

"Yeah, sorry," Emrys said, flicking on his desk lamp. "Lost track of time."

"Serena's outside," his dad said. "She wants to talk to you— in the hall. Everything all right between you two? She seemed a little tense."

Emrys nodded. "Yeah," he said. "Just a disagreement. But we'll work through it."

The expression on his father's face clouded for a moment, but then he gave Emrys a supportive smile. "I know you will," he said gently. "You're both good kids. And I . . . I understand it's hard moving to a new place, Em. Just want you to know that your mom and I see that. But we're also so proud of the effort you've made here. We see that, too. And we're lucky to have such cool neighbors, huh? Hazel and Serena and their families . . ."

"Yeah," Emrys agreed. Then, "But you're pretty cool, too, Dad."

Renner Houtman beamed at his son. "Back at you, buddy. Now, you've got a disagreement to solve and I've got a chicken to roast. Meet back in an hour to turn in our quests and rake in the XP?"

"Definitely," said Emrys.

Edna Milton

From the New Rotterdam Wiki Project

Edna Milton holds the dubious honor of being the only adult suspected of falling victim to the Wandering Hour.

By all accounts, Edna led a largely unremarkable life until her sixties. She was born and raised in New Rotterdam's Shambles Row district in 1903, married a factory worker in 1921, and took a job as a postal clerk in 1930. On March 24, 1940, her husband died by snakebite following Easter services at the First Penitent Church of New Rotterdam, infamous at the time for encouraging its congregation to prove their faith by handling venomous snakes. Strangely, the coroner's report showed no bite wounds.

In 1962, following her retirement, Edna completed a foster parent application with the New Rotterdam Department of Child Welfare. Over the next two years, thirteen different children were placed in her home on a temporary basis.

Five of them disappeared without a trace.

Runaways are all too common in the foster care system, and in the 1960s, it was alarmingly easy for a preteen or teenager to

evade authorities, hitchhike out of the state, and drop off the grid entirely. So, for a time, Edna escaped any blame for the missing children, and she stayed on the department's active roster of foster homes.

Upon the fifth disappearance, however, someone in the department must have finally grown suspicious. Edna's foster license was revoked. The reason given was the presence of a pet that was deemed "potentially dangerous to children." The pet was a large python—an unusual choice of pet, particularly at the time, but it's unclear whether the department saw the animal as a genuine danger or simply used the excuse to sever ties with Edna. Either way, several of the children who had been left in her care went on record about the snake, claiming that Edna threatened to set it loose if they misbehaved. She also told at least two children that "snakes eat their own children" and that the practice "kept them young." (While some snakes do eat their young, pythons are not believed to be among them.)

Following the termination of Edna's license, police informed her that she should not leave town, as a larger investigation was pending. But when officers returned to her apartment the next day, she was gone, as was the python. Edna Milton was never heard from again.

Eventually, the woman was declared legally dead, and in the absence of any next of kin, her belongings were cataloged and earmarked for an estate sale. Among those belongings was a gilded hourglass with red sand, leading some to believe that Edna had fallen prey to the unexplained phenomenon known as the Wandering Hour.

11

Serena was waiting outside his apartment, and Emrys wished it were Hazel instead. It was a harsh thought, maybe, but he was anxious to act on what he'd learned. The hourglass was almost certainly nearby. Maybe on this very block! And every moment it was out there was an *hour* Edna might be hunting some innocent kid.

He fired off a quick text as he walked out of his bedroom: *Someone disappeared yesterday. Laundromat on the corner. Keep an eye out.*

He immediately realized that was a strange way to phrase it, since looking at the hourglass was a tremendously bad idea.

You know what I mean. Be careful. Trust your spooky sense.

Emrys resisted the urge to stare at the screen waiting for a reply, but only because Serena was waiting. He opened the door to see her standing there with her arms crossed. "Hey," she said.

"Hey," Emrys replied. "Is everything okay?"

"No," she answered. "My brother just got back from lacrosse, and he's stinking up the whole apartment. I thought . . . if you still needed help with your, you know, 'homework' . . ."

"I just finished, actually." Emrys tried to sound casual, but he could hear the brittleness in his own voice. Serena's hurtful words were still too fresh.

"Oh, okay," she said. "What did you learn?"

Emrys perked up at that. "Do you really want to know?"

"Probably not," Serena said, sighing. "Sorry. I've got a lot on my 'stuff to process' pile right now. But I was hoping we could talk." At the operatic sounds of Emrys's dad preparing dinner, she added, "Somewhere private."

"Sure," said Emrys. "You want to hang out in my room?"

"I had somewhere else in mind," she said, already turning to go. "Leave the book."

Emrys naturally assumed that Serena would lead him downstairs. Instead, she went up. On the landing midway between Emrys's floor and the next, she put her hands on the bottom edge of a grimy window. She had to strain to open it, but with a bit of exertion, she managed. The early evening tousled Emrys's hair with icy fingers, and he suppressed a shudder.

"After you," said Serena, and after a momentary hesitation, Emrys clambered onto the metal fire escape. He was in the space between buildings. Looking down at the alleyway below, all concrete and piled trash, gave him a rush of vertigo. If he fell, it wouldn't be a pleasant landing.

Serena clambered out beside him, and she went up again, gripping the thin, rickety railing of the fire escape and ascending one careful step at a time. Emrys followed.

The fire escape went all the way to the roof, which was strangely uneven and softer than Emrys would have suspected. It was almost springy beneath his feet, and while the rooftop was enclosed on three sides with a raised ridge, its fourth side was open. Emrys couldn't help imagining rolling right off the edge. He eyed it warily.

Serena walked fearlessly across the bright white surface of the roof, homing in on the solitary pop of color: a vibrant green plant in a terra-cotta pot. She pulled a few small tomatoes from the greenery, handing one to Emrys.

"The only plant I've managed to keep alive inside is a cactus," Serena said. "I'm having better luck up here. Try it."

Emrys popped the tomato into his mouth and bit down. Flavor burst across his tongue—a far cry from the wan, watery taste of the tomatoes from the supermarket.

"Good, right?" said Serena. "There's a whole bunch of people in the neighborhood who use their rooftops for gardening. You can see a few of them from here. They aren't growing, like, potion ingredients or man-eating fly traps. They're growing cucumbers and strawberries and basil. Look there."

Serena pointed, and Emrys peered into the distance. New Rotterdam spread out before them, lit by the fading glow of the setting sun. He saw dozens of townhouses and apartment buildings just like theirs; he saw the early evening traffic, backed up at the major intersections around the Shallows, and the holes in the skylines where the city's scattered parks, gardens, and cemeteries crouched between buildings. Beyond it all, he could see a shadowy strip of ocean, its outline framed by distant lighthouses that shone like the first stars in the growing dark of the eastern sky.

"You see that basketball court?" Serena asked. "That's where my brother, Dom, broke his leg when he was trying to climb to the top of the hoop. It's one of my earliest memories. I was so scared when it happened that *Dom* had to comfort *me*. And there." She pointed at a church steeple. "That's the church where my dad took us to help out with a food drive. They told him that his 'lifestyle' would make people uncomfortable. I avoided walking past it for *years* because I didn't trust myself to not throw a rock right through their gaudy window."

"That's awful," said Emrys.

Serena shook her head. "It's depressingly average, actually," she said. "Just your run-of-the-mill ignorance. The everyday kind of evil. And that's my point." She swept an arm out to encompass the city. "New Rotterdam is my home. It's where I took piano lessons and came in second place in a soapbox derby and where I threw up on the boardwalk when I ate too much cotton candy. They wouldn't tell you that on a ghost tour or on *America's Most Haunted* or on that ridiculous *wiki*. But there's more to this town than ghosts and goblins."

Emrys nodded solemnly. "That's true," he said. "But maybe that's *why* we can't ignore what we've learned. Because there are normal people—kids like Brian Skupp—who got caught up in something that they can't understand."

"*Normal* people," Serena echoed, and she sighed, sitting cross-legged on the roof. "I'm sorry I called you . . . what I called you. That was too far, and I didn't mean it."

Emrys lowered himself to sit beside her. "I mean, I *am* weird. I'm learning to accept it about myself. But it hurt, coming from you with so much . . . venom behind it."

"I'm sorry," Serena said again. "In that moment, I think I *wanted* to be hurtful. And then I got home, and I imagined telling Hazel what had happened, and I thought about how she would get my version of the story and your version. And I realized there wasn't really a version where what I said to you was justified. She'd definitely take your side again."

Emrys felt a little guilty, hearing her put it that way. This is why he'd tried so hard to befriend Serena. He didn't want to be a wedge. "I don't want Hazel to have to choose sides," he said.

"Yeah, I know. Me neither." She smiled. "Although it's kind of funny, how she's basically playing the peacemaker even in my head. She's so good at it. And for what it's worth, I'm totally down with the idea that *weird* can be a good thing."

"I hope so," Emrys said. He thought of Van Stavern's words. "If I can embrace what makes me different . . . if I can *wield* it . . . then maybe I can help people. People who want New Rotterdam to be a sleepy seaside town where the only monsters they'll encounter are the stuffed souvenirs from the gift shops."

"People like me?" Serena said, and though it sounded like a question, it didn't seem to be one she was directing at Emrys. "I'll be honest. I wish I never saw that place—the reliquary or whatever it's called. I wish I'd stayed home that night." She shook her head. "But Hazel was going after you, and I couldn't let her do it alone. So I can't say I'd do anything differently. But ever since that night . . . I'm so *scared*, Emrys. I don't like being scared."

Emrys grinned. "I don't think anybody *likes* being scared."

She drew her legs up, hugging her knees to her chest. "But when I'm scared, I panic. I do stupid things, like pulling a buzzer off the wall. Or saying mean things to a nice guy who just wants to help people."

Emrys blushed, the compliment somehow just as uncomfortable for him as her earlier insult had been.

"I don't know what I'd do if something actually bad happened," she continued. "Like if what happened to Mr. Pierce happened to me? I wouldn't last five seconds."

"I know what you mean," Emrys said. "And, just so you know, I'm scared, too." He met her eyes. "I'm scared pretty much all the time. But I think maybe the thing I'm most afraid of is doing nothing."

Serena didn't say anything for a little while. Emrys wondered if he should have said something different, or if maybe she was expecting him to say something more now. But he stayed quiet, stewing in his discomfort, until Serena finally broke the silence, declaring, "I'm cold. Let's go back inside."

It was fully dark now, and the streetlights below did little to light their descent down the fire escape. Emrys felt no small amount of relief when he set his feet down on the inside stairwell. Serena eased herself through the open window behind him. There was a quiet confidence in her movements and a subtle fierceness in how she held her chin. Despite her confession, she still appeared fearless to him.

He was glad they'd cleared the air. Falling into step beside her, he felt himself stand a little straighter. Even if she *was* scared—and even if she refused to involve herself with the Order more than she already had—Emrys felt more sure of himself, knowing that she didn't resent him. He turned to wish her good night.

And heard her let out a sudden whimper.

"Oh . . . oh, *no*," Serena said, her eyes fixed on the landing below them.

Emrys followed her gaze. There on the landing sat a beautiful ornate hourglass, its top bulb filled with red sand.

Q Search New Rotterdam Wiki

Talk: The Wandering Hour

From the New Rotterdam Wiki Project

> This is the talk page for discussing improvements to the the Wandering Hour article.

> This is not a forum for general discussion of the article's subject.

Edna's kids?

Is it worth naming the kids who went missing under Edna's care? Do we have those records? Maybe set up a list page?
@TheRotterFiles (user) 14:04, 5 May [reply]

Definitely worth it. But while we have the number, unfortunately the names have been lost. If anyone even bothered noting them at all. @LongNeckedDoug (user) 14:32, 5 May [reply]

There's that great NR Police Department record-keeping we know and love! @TheRotterFiles (user) 14:50, 5 May [reply]

Poor kids... @BlackthorneBabe (user) 22:05, 13 August [reply]

What happened to Biff Bentley?

"Biff lived the rest of his life under the suspicion that he had murdered the love of his life." What happened to this guy? Does this mean he died? @MadrettorWen (user) 09:43, 23 June [reply]

Heart attack. Just added a line to the end of the paragraph. @LongNeckedDoug (user) 11:01, 24 June [reply]

Scary!

I gotta say, this is probably the scariest creepypasta I've encountered on this wiki. Imagine just DISAPPEARING and never being seen again. If not for the handful of survivors who told their stories, we'd never even know to connect the dots. And at least one of them got committed?? Also: SNAKES! @BlackthorneBabe (user) 22:21, 13 August [reply]

This page isn't for general discussion, Blackthorne. Feel free to join the **StrifeChat** server for that. @LongNeckedDoug (user) 08:05, 14 August [reply]

...but yes. It's definitely one of the worst. And even scarier because we know so little. All I can say is, if you ever spot a strange hourglass—*run*. And don't *stop* running. @LongNeckedDoug (user) 08:11, 14 August [reply]

Godspeed everyone! @AmberBishop (user) 13:48, 14 August [reply]

12

Emrys quickly averted his gaze from the red-sand hour-glass. He turned to Serena, who stared back at him, her eyes wide with horror. "I saw it first," she said, her voice thick with fear.

Emrys knew with dreadful clarity what would happen next. He would blink, and Serena would be gone, disappearing like a shadow in sunlight. For him, only a moment would pass, but she would endure a cruel and lonesome hour. An hour in which she would be hunted. Taunted. Devoured.

Less than an hour, maybe. *I wouldn't last five seconds.*

It would happen right under Emrys's nose, and he would be powerless to stop it. As powerless as Biff Bentley had been when his girlfriend, Betty, had seen the hourglass a moment before he had.

Although . . . Enoch Pierce hadn't been helpless. Emrys's mind began to race in the few seconds Serena had left.

Enoch had been able to hide in the water, which continued to flow even though the water should have been solid, frozen in time as surely as if it had been ice. Because Enoch had been in contact with the water. Just like he'd been in contact with the football helmet! He'd been able to take the helmet with him into the Wandering Hour and wield it like a weapon. His mistake had been in letting it go when he threw it at Edna Milton.

Emrys lunged out and grabbed Serena's wrist. She startled, pulling away instinctively, but he gripped her even tighter. "Hold on to me!" he said. "Don't let go even for a second."

It was then that the sand in the hourglass began to trickle down in a steady streak of red. As the relic became unstuck in time, everything else froze. Emrys could tell by the sudden absence of the ever-present buzz of the electric lights. The color of that light seemed to shift, as if a veil had settled between Emrys and his surroundings.

Serena gasped, and Emrys felt a thrill of relief. His hunch had been right! Contact with Serena had brought him into the Wandering Hour right beside her. Whatever happened next, they would face it together.

It was the thought of *whatever happened next* that instantly quelled his enthusiasm.

A creak came from the floor above—Van Stavern's ruined apartment. In the utter silence that surrounded them, it sounded impossibly loud—and the threat it carried wrapped Emrys's heart in icy tendrils.

He willed himself to be silent and still. He could feel Serena do the same.

As they watched, a shadow unfurled above them, stretching across the wall farther up the stairwell. It was a human figure—or it appeared human, anyway.

"Serena, dear?" called a voice, kindly and frail. "Is that you?"

A shudder of terror and revulsion traveled through Serena's body and up Emrys's arm. His grip was clammy against her skin.

"What do we do?" Serena whispered, so quiet her words were almost lost in the sound of her trembling breath.

"*Run*," said Emrys.

They bounded down the narrow staircase hand in hand, hurtling past the hourglass. Red sand slid between the glass bulbs, unhurriedly counting the seconds as Emrys and Serena scrambled for their lives.

"Oh my, Serena, you've brought a friend along!" Edna Milton called from above, a spark of excitement touching her brittle voice. "It's been quite a while since anyone thought of *that*."

A crash echoed down from the penthouse floor. Something astonishingly large and heavy glided toward them, its weight shaking the whole building.

Emrys made a hard turn. His shoulder scraped against the wall, but he was careful to keep his hand linked with Serena's. One slip and she would disappear forever.

They passed Emrys's apartment, where his mom was leaving to walk the dog before dinner. Grace Houtman stooped over

Sir Galahound, who was frozen in excitement, his front paws suspended in the air.

The sight of his mother sent a hitch through Emrys's chest. He wanted to call out to her, to beg her to save them. Maybe if he and Serena touched her, they could bring her into the Hour, too.

And then? What could even a grown-up possibly do against something as impossible and horrible as this? And what kind of danger might Emrys be exposing his mother to by dragging her into Edna's twisted game? He and Serena needed to hide. Their only chance was in waiting out the time limit.

Down and down they careened, Emrys jostling against the building walls, Serena gripping the rail for balance with her free hand. All the while, the heavy slithering weight drew closer. Soon they reached Serena's floor—just as a dark shape occluded the light above them.

"In!" Serena screamed, slamming open the door to her apartment with a shoulder check. She dashed inside, yanking Emrys behind her. Together, the two of them flung the door closed.

Serena quickly slid the dead bolt into place, huffing with fear and exertion. "What do we do? Oh god, Emrys. I don't . . . I can't . . ."

Emrys frantically took in the space, looking for a place to hide. Serena's whole family was home—each of them frozen in time. Her dads were in the kitchen, Mr. Navarro preparing dinner while Mr. Dubose poured two glasses of wine. A glittering braid of magenta hung suspended between the bottle and glass like a liquid garland.

Serena's brother, Dom, reclined on the couch, still half-dressed in his lacrosse clothes. His hand was raised with the remote pointed at the TV, where Mayor Royce's face loomed large on the screen. Apparently he'd been in the process of muting it.

"Is she still out there?" Serena asked. "Do you think she saw us come in?"

Emrys pressed his ear against the door. He didn't hear anything.

But whatever had been chasing them was immense. Shouldn't he hear something?

Then, the eerie sound of laughter—high and light and fragile as a glass bell. Except it wasn't coming from outside.

It was coming from Serena's bedroom.

As Emrys and Serena both snapped around, a figure emerged from the doorway: a wizened old woman in a delicate knit sweater.

At first glance, Edna Milton looked for all the world like a harmless granny. But Emrys didn't need the Order's second sight to sense the menace that lurked behind that disguise. She moved in a strange, circuitous track, and her bewildered smile couldn't quite conceal the hunger in her gaze.

"You can run, dear," the woman said, in the permissive tone of an elder indulging a rambunctious child. "And you can even hide. But I can *always* follow, Serena."

Edna smiled, and her lips split open too wide. The skin along her cheeks tore along hidden seams, a mask that was pulling apart.

Emrys realized the hourglass had appeared as well. Its tortured golden frame towered from atop the kitchen counter, red sand sliding into its transparent belly. Barely any, compared to what occupied the upper bulb.

Such little time had passed. How would they possibly escape Edna for the full hour?

Serena screamed. She lunged toward where her brother sat on the sofa—and the metal lacrosse stick that was propped against it.

With a jolt of panic, Emrys felt his slick palm losing its grip on her hand. He couldn—

The sensation that followed was among the most unpleasant experiences of his life. The world dilated, like a film reel going slack. Noises warped, Serena's war-bellow pitching low and slow. Emrys could even feel his own racing heartbeat stretching in his chest.

Then everything contracted again, the film coming back into speed. Emrys was yanked in the other direction, his almost comically low yelp rising in pitch as he caught up with time.

It was a dizzying, profoundly disturbing ordeal. One moment, he'd been scrambling to keep up with Serena—farther into the apartment—while now she was pulling him out the door in the other direction.

Serena must have dropped his hand for a moment, freezing him in time with the rest of the world.

"I can only help you if you hold on!" he shouted, just hoping he wouldn't trip in his disorientation.

"I tried to break the hourglass!" Serena huffed. "But it's too tough. My brother's stick didn't leave a scratch!"

They pitched down another floor, Emrys's head still spinning. Apparently a closed apartment wouldn't be enough. They had to find another place to hide. There was no time to reach the water, as Enoch Pierce had. But where else could they go?

It's important that you're able to access the reliquary at all times.

Van Stavern's lesson from earlier that day rang through Emrys's thoughts.

Anywhere you find a door, you can find an entrance.

"Wait!" Emrys screamed, digging his heel into the landing and holding Serena's wrist for dear life as she attempted to keep sprinting toward the next staircase. "A door! I need a door!"

"A *what*?!" Serena shouted. Her eyes were wild with panic.

Emrys stared at the nearest doorway to one of his neighbor's apartments. Van Stavern had promised that any door would do. Emrys scoured his memory for the incantation Van Stavern had given him into the Order's magical reliquary.

Then he looked down at the hand currently gripping Serena's wrist.

Ostiarius aperi was written in clear black Sharpie across his forearm.

A heavy thud shook the landing above. The old woman's laughter broke out again, but it sounded wrong this time. Each peal warped and whistled, deforming to a ragged, wet hiss.

"Emrys, we have to *go!*" Serena pleaded. She tried to tug Emrys away, but he held his ground—nearly breaking their grip for a terrifying beat.

"But what's the last word?" he wondered aloud. "P-something. Portal? Puerto?"

Serena gazed down at the writing. "That's Latin . . ." she said. "Accusative case would be . . . is it *portam?*"

Emrys gasped as the word slotted into his memory. He pressed his free palm to the door. "*Ostiarius aperi portam!*" he shouted.

Just like in the bathroom, gooseflesh rose all along Emrys's arms. His right eye buzzed with anticipatory energy. By Serena's sudden hushed pause, he guessed she felt it, too.

He lunged for the door handle—a handle that should surely have been locked—and found that it clicked easily open. Emrys pushed the door, revealing the same sprawling, otherworldly chamber he and his friends had stumbled into when this all began.

Serena looked appropriately shocked, but didn't waste a moment clambering inside. Emrys quickly followed, throwing the door shut behind him.

He and Serena stood before the reliquary's grand spire of an entrance, the brass doorknob regarding them coolly with its blue enamel eye.

Emrys bent over, panting, willing his head to stop spinning. Still, he didn't dare break contact with Serena, who was herself now backing away from the door.

"Van Stavern said . . . this place was . . . safe," Emrys gasped. "Taught me how to get in."

Serena's shoulders unhitched a bit at that, but the fear hadn't left her expression. "How does he know, though? He'd never even heard of the Wandering Hour before today, right?"

"I'm not sure this place *exists* in the real world," Emrys said. "How could she possibly follow us here?"

Serena shook her head. "Emrys, you heard that thing. She said she could follow me *anywhere*."

"And what a *wonderful* site you've led me to, Serena."

The Yellow Court

From the New Rotterdam Wiki Project

The New Rotterdam Wiki Project does not have an article with this exact name. You may want to check your spelling, or search for your query under an alternate name.

If you have been linked to this page from another article, please delete the faulty link and any accompanying text.

Your privacy settings have been reset.

Location services have been activated. Your IP address has been logged.

Do not answer the door.

13

Every nerve in Emrys's body fired at the same time. His legs shook ferociously, and his breath caught in his lungs. Edna's voice echoed from everywhere at once.

"No," Serena moaned, her voice thick with despair. "Please, no . . ."

Emrys caught sight of the hourglass looming on the reliquary's mantle, the thin line of blood-red sand spooling down, down, down in its ever-patient pursuit.

Serena had been right yet again. Somehow, the Wandering Hour had found them even here. If they couldn't hide in the reliquary, where would they ever be safe?

"A space outside of space," Edna's voice crooned. "A time outside of time. We're something of a matching set, aren't we?" Emrys caught a glimpse of a large shadow undulating between the relic pedestals, but it moved too fast for him to see clearly.

"I could hunt anywhere I liked from here, now, couldn't I?" Edna said. "No assistance necessary. And so many interesting bric-a-bracs." Her voice was disturbingly hollow—a wide glass jar that had been gradually emptied and was now ready for refilling.

"Okay," Serena said softly. "Okay. No more panic. No more running."

Emrys glanced at his friend. The fear had finally left Serena's expression, replaced by a look he liked even less.

"I'm sorry, Emrys," Serena murmured. She wouldn't meet his eyes. "For everything. Maybe if I'd just accepted all this from the beginning, things would have been different."

Emrys followed her gaze to the glittering shield on its pedestal—the relic she'd been studying the night before. He felt her posture shift as she prepared to run for it.

"No," Emrys rasped, shaking his head and tightening his grip. "Serena, *no*. Don't let go. I can't help you if you let go!"

"Always trying to help the unhelpable," Serena said with a sigh. "It's your most annoying quality."

But when her eyes finally found his, they were bright with tears.

"Tell Hazel I didn't make it easy."

"SERENA, N—"

The world distended again, time swelling as Serena wrenched herself free of his grip. Emrys's plea stretched like starlight crossing the cold expanse of the universe, a pinpoint of heat and brilliance pulled so taut it lost its shape. Its purpose.

The plea floated listlessly, suspended in a frozen infinity.

Until, as a hand latched *hard* onto his ankle, time snapped violently back into place.

"—OHHH!"

Emrys was wrenched from his feet, his head cracking against the reliquary's marble floor. The world exploded into a white-hot supernova of pain, Emrys's field of vision suddenly *full* of shimmering stars.

The reliquary had changed.

Many of the plinths were toppled, their dangerous artifacts spilled haphazardly across the floor. The rug at the center of the sitting space now appeared to be on fire, and the warm, comfortable hues of the room were replaced by flickering shadows.

Emrys's head swam. His eyes barely caught a hazy shape in the background. An enormous pale mouth opened wider than any human mouth should, and inside it . . .

Inside it . . . !

"EMRYS!"

Emrys realized that someone was screaming his name—had been screaming it this whole time. His eyes focused on Serena: on her fearful gaze, and the hand gripping his ankle, and the legs that were half-swallowed by a gigantic gullet now writhing from the darkness.

His eyes unfocused again. His head hurt *so much*. As his thoughts spun, he caught glimpses of the reliquary: a toppled bookshelf, an oaken table scored by flames, and above it all, a pristine hourglass untouched by the carnage. Slowly counting— slowly, slowly.

Emrys raised his hand toward the hourglass, as if he might grasp it from even this far.

He couldn't think. He couldn't *focus*.

You have an unquiet mind.

Serena! Serena needed him! But what could he do for her? He wasn't a sorcerer. He couldn't speak ancient languages or calculate otherworldly equations. He was just a weird kid who'd stumbled onto a facet of the world that was so much bigger and darker than even he'd ever dreamed of.

That word again.

The weird is ours to wield.

"EMRYS!"

Serena screamed his name again. She was being *eaten alive* and there was nothing he could . . .

It wants to tell a story—a strange story—and true mastery is just about letting it tell that story through you.

The stars twinkling in Emrys's field of vision began to stretch, pulling into glittering strands that hung in the air like smoldering spiderwebs.

Wield the weird.

Wield the weird.

The phrase looped through Emrys's addled thoughts, again and again. Slowly, he realized he wasn't just thinking the words—he was saying them, unconsciously repeating the phrase like a mantra . . .

"Wield . . . the . . . weird."

Or like an incantation.

All across the room, the glittering strands shivered with excitement. Something was coming—they sensed it. Something *momentous*.

"Wield . . ." Emrys said, his voice heavy with strange authority. He pictured the Atlas and its blinking eye. Willed the relic to help him save his friend.

" . . . the . . ."

The strands brightened. The light was dazzling, ecstatic. Emrys could *feel* them parting—a curtain pulling wide.

"*WEIRD.*"

The air between Emrys and the hourglass warped like twisted fabric. It was as if that small weft of reality were just a layer of silk that could be easily swept aside by a deft hand. Alien colors shimmered between its folds, light peering through from some other impossible source. The colors were beautiful and awful—they whispered to Emrys of forbidden questions with terrifying answers. A torrent of eldritch energy poured over the hourglass, tongues of eerie brightness licking the bulbs.

The glass cracked.

As slowly as the red sand poured down, a single line spread up from the lower bulb, across its narrow throat, and toward the golden rim.

Then, with a sound like a hundred voices screaming, the glass shattered. A sea of red sand spilled onto the reliquary's marble floor. It poured from the broken relic, whipping through the space with the ferocity of a sudden storm until the air was full of crimson whirlwinds. Emrys's spell and its strange energies were completely consumed.

Now there truly *was* screaming, he was sure of it. Emrys saw bizarre figures rising in the storm, dozens of humanoid shapes molded from red sand. They lurched unhurriedly past him, reaching for something or someone beyond his field of vision.

Serena's grip was yanked from his ankle—but this time the world didn't stop.

"*Serena!*" he screamed.

"Emrys!" she called back over the din.

"Help mee-*EEE!*" a third, eerily hollow voice echoed in the distance.

They were Edna's reedy howls, but her voice grew harder to hear with each passing moment, as if she were being dragged away.

And then, as abruptly as it had begun, the storm was over. The winds subsided, and ruby sand drifted slowly to the floor. The room grew thunderously quiet.

Emrys whirled around to find Serena was just behind him, terrified but unharmed. Her wide brown eyes gazed back at him from beneath a layer of fine red dust.

Edna Milton was never heard from again.

EPILOGUE

It was an unseasonably warm afternoon in New Rotterdam. The sun, which had been wan and pale all week, burned with renewed intensity, dispelling the city's ubiquitous fog. It was as if nature itself had taken notice of Emrys and Serena's victory over the Wandering Hour and found it fit to celebrate.

Or maybe it was just due to global warming.

It had been less than a full day since Serena had been half-devoured by a monster with the face of an old woman, and despite their exhaustion and shock, none of them wanted to be indoors. Serena, in particular, couldn't bear to be in her apartment, where the memory of the red hourglass was too vivid, as unconquerable in her mind's eye as it had been when she'd tried with all her might to shatter it.

Emrys recognized her need to assert some control over her fear; to get up and *do* something, however small.

And so they were honoring the dead.

The adults of New Rotterdam would likely never know what had happened to Edna Milton's victims. As Enoch Pierce had learned the hard way, adults didn't really *want* the truth if it didn't conform to their preconceived ideas about how the world worked:

Monsters weren't real.

The people in power could be trusted to take care of things.

The tragedies that befell other people's families couldn't happen to them.

But Emrys, Hazel, and Serena didn't have the luxury of embracing those comforting lies. And they couldn't let the names of the dead remain unspoken.

They spoke Casper Jennings's name at the laundromat and Betty Grimm's in Arcadia Park. They read Emma Winthrop's poem aloud, and, just outside the fence of Gideon de Ruiter Middle School, they watched a video of a band performance the school had posted online the year before. Brian Skupp had a tuba solo. Emrys thought he was pretty good.

Their path home brought them through the Shallows.

"We should tell Mr. Pierce what happened," Emrys suggested. "He deserves to know. He was her victim, too, after all."

Hazel touched his shoulder. "You're right," she said. "That's good of you to think of him."

She'd been handling Emrys with kid gloves all morning, offering gentle words of affirmation and even offering to do his chores. It was as if she thought he might crumble to dust at the slightest provocation, and he couldn't say for certain that she was wrong.

"I think you missed your chance," Serena said flatly, and Emrys looked over to where she stood, just outside Mr. Pierce's antique store.

The display window out front, which had previously been home to a chaotic assortment of knickknacks, was now empty except for a single sign. It read: RETAIL SPACE FOR RENT.

"That happened fast," said Hazel. "Even for the Shallows."

Serena pushed the door. It was unlocked, swinging open and setting off the bell.

A few days ago, Emrys would have hesitated, fearful of trespassing, as he had when they'd stood outside Van Stavern's ruined apartment. Today, he stepped forward without a second thought, slipping past Serena and into the shadowy shop interior. The cheerful bell echoed in the empty space.

The wreckage of apartment #701 had awed Emrys into momentary silence, and the utter vacantness of the one-time antique shop had the same effect. There had been so much *stuff* packed in there less than twenty-four hours ago. Now, if not for the trails and treads marring a thick layer of dust, someone might think the space had been deserted for ages.

"I don't understand," he said at last. "It's completely empty."

"Not quite," Hazel said, pushing past him. "Look."

Emrys saw it then. Atop the glass display case in the center of the room was a small figurine set beside a handwritten note.

Hazel got there first. She held the note tightly with both hands, as if it might slip through her fingers. "It's addressed to you, Serena."

Serena took the note, unfolding it while Emrys watched over her shoulder. The note read:

I'm sorry.

I didn't have a choice. The end is here, and it is hungry.

One day, you'll understand.

Serena made a choking sound, and she brought her hand up to her mouth. It took Emrys a moment to realize she was crying. Hazel reached for her, but Serena held up her hand and shook her head. *Don't.*

"I don't understand," said Hazel. "Why is he sorry?"

Emrys lifted the small figurine gingerly between his index finger and thumb. His skin prickled, but he couldn't tell if it was due to a supernatural sixth sense or plain old intuition.

"And what is that?" asked Hazel.

"It's a chess piece," Emrys answered.

Hazel's brow furrowed. "Chess pieces are supposed to be white or black. Why is it yellow?"

"Not just yellow," Emrys said flatly. In fact, the figurine was almost golden in color—a rich, warm hue that was as sunny as the day outside. It made Emrys sick. Pieces began shifting in his mind, a chess game Emrys and his friends hadn't even realized they'd been playing—been losing—all along.

"It's amber," he said. "It's an *amber bishop*."

As in @AmberBishop. Emrys had spoken with someone using that online handle just the other night.

He looked up at his friends. "Enoch Pierce is an admin on the wiki. And I think . . . I think this means . . ."

He turned the piece over. Inscribed on the bottom were two letters in an elegant, looping script.

$$\mathcal{YC}$$

"It means he's with the Yellow Court."

Emrys wasn't surprised to discover that @AmberBishop's account had been discontinued. Enoch Pierce had vacated the digital realm as hastily as he'd cleared out of his shop.

Emrys wasn't sure if that had been by choice. Had Mr. Pierce simply gone into hiding before the kids could bring him to account for his crimes? Had he retreated deeper into the sheltering shadows of the Yellow Court? Or had he been taken off the board, punished by his collaborators for the loss of a one-of-a-kind relic?

Emrys couldn't know the answer to that or any of his other questions. He believed Pierce truly had survived a harrowing encounter with Edna Milton in his youth. He also felt certain that Pierce had been the one leaving the hourglass where it would be found by unsuspecting victims, allowing Edna to hunt. But what would drive a man to subject other innocent people to a horror he himself had barely survived? What could the Yellow Court possibly have offered him? How could anyone be so selfish and cruel?

One day, you'll understand.

Emrys shuddered at the thought. He hoped Pierce was wrong about that.

×

"You've seen now what happens when the wrong relic falls into the wrong hands," said Van Stavern. "Monsters are the result."

"Are you talking about Edna Milton?" asked Emrys. "Or about Enoch Pierce?"

"Both," said Van Stavern. "Monsters wear many skins. And some walk among us."

"The better to shove us into oncoming traffic," Serena said sullenly.

They'd gathered in the reliquary, where Van Stavern had briefly praised them on their victory—before seeing the full extent of the damage and directing them to set things right at once. Although she bore the least blame for the state of the place, Hazel spearheaded the restoration efforts, spurred on by her obvious guilt.

"I can't believe I missed the whole thing," she said. "If anything had happened to you—to *either* of you . . ."

"It isn't your fault," said Serena. "That's all there is to it."

"You did miss a bit of sand, though," said Emrys. "Over by the suit of armor."

There had been a *lot* of sand to sweep up, and broken glass, and the place still smelled faintly of smoke. But Van Stavern confirmed that nothing had been irreparably damaged—aside from the hourglass, of course.

"You know," said the book, "standard procedure is to secure the relics for containment and study. Not to destroy them."

"Sorry, not sorry," said Serena. "Now are you going to teach Hazel and me this portal spell, or what?"

Emrys perked up at that. "Does that mean . . . ?"

"That I'm joining your monster-hunting club?" said Serena. "A monster swallowed my *shoe* last night, Emrys. I think I'm in the club whether I like it or not."

"I'm glad," said Hazel. "I wouldn't want to do it without you."

To Emrys's surprise, he didn't feel a pang of jealousy hearing Hazel say that. In fact, he realized he agreed with the sentiment entirely.

"Hold on," he said. "You need to make it official."

Serena sighed, but she didn't argue. She didn't even hesitate. She strode over to the nearby pedestal, lifting the gleaming shield as if she'd intended to do so all along. "It's lighter than it looks. But heavier, too." She slid the shield onto her arm, then turned back in their direction. "If it helps keep us safe, then I'll carry it."

"It suits you, truth-seeker," said Van Stavern.

Emrys grinned. He didn't know precisely what Van Stavern meant by the epithet, but the shield *did* suit her. And when he saw himself and Hazel reflected on its surface, they didn't look like scared little kids. They looked capable and determined.

"Now, the spell," said Van Stavern. "It will allow you immediate access to the Blue Reliquary—"

"The Doomsday Archives," said Emrys.

"Come again?"

"We should call it the Doomsday Archives, like on the wiki. After all, if we're the last remaining members of the Order, then we should find our own way into the story. And I think the wiki will be a big part of that. We're going to need every advantage we can get—the relics, sure, but more modern tools, too."

Van Stavern fixed him with his single watery eye. "Right you are, Emrys," he said. "I can see the Order is in fine hands. If you three are our future . . . then there is hope for us yet."

✕

The next time they gathered for movie night, they decided to take a break from horror. There was no shortage of superhero movies, with predictable plotlines and uncomplicated morality. And happy endings, of course. Emrys decided he could do with more of those.

Before Serena could launch her streaming app of choice, her TV defaulted to a local news channel. Mayor Royce stood at a podium, flanked by two men. One was lanky, with a sadistic sharpness to his features; the other was squat with hooded eyes. *A fly trap and a pitcher plant.* They were the police detectives that Emrys and Hazel had seen at their school. The air of menace they'd exuded that day wasn't at all softened by the television. Royce, for his part, seemed utterly at ease before the assembled reporters, despite the antagonistic relationship between the mayor and the press. Emrys swore he could see the contempt in the man's smile, the sneer of a playground bully with powerful parents who could indulge every cruel impulse without fear of reprisal or consequences.

The text at the bottom of the screen revealed that Royce was suspending the city's recycling program. "Ultimately, this will free up resources that can be better allocated to initiatives that truly *matter* to taxpayers," he said.

"I hope the taxpayers know how to swim," Serena said, her voice dripping with sarcasm.

"Ugh, hurry up and change the channel," Emrys said. People had actually voted for him? How could anyone fail to see him for what he really was?

"Hold on," said Hazel. "Do you see that?"

"Ow," Serena said, rubbing her eye.

Slowly, Emrys realized their second sight had kicked in. But why? What had triggered it this time? He gazed around the apartment, waiting for the Midtown Mummy to leap out of the shadows—or some new evil artifact to emerge, bent on swallowing them whole.

Then he took another look at the TV, and he gasped.

How could anyone fail to see him for what he really was? That's what Emrys had wondered.

So what was he?

Emrys didn't know. But as he and Hazel and Serena stared slack-jawed at the TV, he swore the mayor was staring back at them, his shark eyes glinting with malice.

On his lapel, he wore a small pin in the shape of a chess piece. It was a yellow king.

ACKNOWLEDGMENTS

One of our favorite things to discuss during school and library visits is the exciting potential that comes from cooperative storytelling. Creating art with others invites an electric, unpredictable sort of sorcery and makes the process feel a bit less lonely. In a series that aims to explore our anxieties about the world, that's been doubly important for the both of us.

But in truth, every book that goes through a publisher is a cooperative venture. Often there are unsung heroes helping to shape the story whose names never appear on the cover. So we'd like to take a moment to sing their praises ourselves.

First and foremost, thanks to Tiffany Liao, our inspired and inspiring editor. What can we even say? Your enthusiasm for this project has been the beacon that guided us through New Rotterdam's foggy seas. Thank you for your patience as we found our footing and for your wise, generous, big-hearted counsel during the drafting process. You had a clear vision for this series, even when we were stumbling through the dark. We can't thank you enough for taking a chance on us, or for the deft hand you had in shaping this book into everything it could be.

That goes for everyone on the Zando team, as well. What an absolute gift it's been working with this bright and energetic crew of people. TJ Ohler, thank you for your brilliant insights and endless patience. Thanks to the publicity and marketing teams who absolutely blew us away with their enthusiasm and creativity, especially Associate Publicist Sara Hayet and Director of Publicity Chloe Texier-Rose, and Marketing Coordinator Amelia Olsen, Senior Marketing Manager Allegra Green, Associate Director of Digital Strategy Anna Hall, and Director of Marketing and Imprint Partnerships Nathalie Ramirez.

Thank you to the small army of sages who kept us and this book on track: Copy Editor Rachel Kowal, Managing Editor and Production Manager Sarah Schneider, and Associate Production Editor and Contracts Coordinator Jed Munson. And to the team at Neuwirth, Managing Editor Jeff Farr, Managing Editorial Assistant Noah Perkins, Production Associate Lexi Winter, and Production Director Beth Metrick. And to Director of Rights Sierra Stovall and Head of Sales Andrew Rein, for your work getting this out to readers far and wide. And a huge thank you to Zando's CEO Molly Stern for allowing us to be among the first middle-grade projects Zando publishes. We are absolutely humbled by the honor.

The package! This gorgeous package! That's all due to designer extraordinaire Carol Ly, Art Director Evan Gaffney, and to the incredible artists who leant us their talents, cover artist Chris Shehan and interior artist Julian Callos.

A huge thank you to our agents Ammi-Joan Pacquette (for Zack) and Josh and Tracey Adams (for Nick). Your support over the years has been invaluable. And thanks, as always, to David Levithan, who has championed us in more ways than we can count.

Thank you to our husbands, Zack Lewis and Andrew Eliopulos. You make navigating these scary seas a little less daunting. And to Nick's new son, Theodore Calob James Eliopulos—your smile is bright enough to scorch away any fog. You will always have loving allies in the journeys ahead.

Lastly, thanks to you, our readers. Magic wants to tell a story, a *strange* story, and that makes you a part of this telling. We're so grateful that you joined us.

ABOUT THE AUTHORS

Zack Loran Clark and Nick Eliopulos are best friends with a shared love of roleplaying games, epic fantasy, and spooky stories. Together, they are the authors of The Adventurers Guild trilogy. Separately, Zack is the author of *The Lock-Eater*, and Nick has written more than a dozen officially licensed Minecraft books. Zack lives in Brooklyn, where he keeps a collection of potentially mystical artifacts. Nick lives in Upstate New York, beside an allegedly haunted river. Thanks to the wonders of the internet, they still game together every week.

The thrills continue . . .

Keep your eye out for
more adventures in